DON'T GO TO SLEEP IN THE DARK

Don't Go to Sleep in the Dark

Short Stories

CELIA FREMLIN

ff

FABER & FABER

This edition first published in 2014
by Faber and Faber Ltd
Bloomsbury House, 74–77 Great Russell Street
London WC1B 3DA

All rights reserved
© Celia Fremlin, 1968, 1969, 1970
Preface © Chris Simmons, 2014

The right of Celia Fremlin to be identified
as author of this work has been asserted in accordance
with Section 77 of the Copyright, Designs and Patents Act 1988

The following stories have appeared in *Ellery Queen's Mystery Magazine*: 'The Locked Room', 'The Special Gift', 'Angel-Face', 'The New House'; 'The Quiet Game' has appeared in *She*; 'Last Day of Spring' has appeared in *Best Mystery Stories* edited by Maurice Richardson.

This book is sold subject to the condition that it shall not, by way of
trade or otherwise, be lent, resold, hired out or otherwise circulated
without the publisher's prior consent in any form of binding or cover other than
that in which it is published and without a similar condition including this
condition being imposed on the subsequent purchaser

A CIP record for this book is available from the British Library

ISBN 978-0-571-31271-9

CONTENTS

Preface to the 2014 Edition	vii
The Quiet Game	1
The Betrayal	11
The New House	18
Last Day of Spring	35
The Special Gift	41
Old Daniel's Treasure	56
For Ever Fair	67
The Irony of Fate	78
The Baby-Sitter	92
The Hated House	104
Angel-Face	115
The Fated Interview	127
The Locked Room	139

Preface to the 2014 Edition

Celia Fremlin was born in Kingsbury, Middlesex, on 20 June 1914, to Heaver and Margaret Fremlin. Her father was a doctor, and she spent her childhood in Hertfordshire before going on to study at Oxford. Between 1958 and 1994 she published sixteen novels of suspense and three collections of stories, highly acclaimed in their day. Sadly, Fremlin's work had largely fallen out of print by the time I discovered her for myself in the mid-1990s. But I was captivated by the elegant, razor-sharp quality of her writing and – as often when one finds an author one is passionate about – keen to learn more about the writer's life. Then, in early 2005, I had the great good fortune of having several conversations with Celia Fremlin's elder daughter Geraldine Goller. Geraldine was a charming woman and I found our discussions enlightening, helping me to understand Celia Fremlin better and to appreciate why she wrote the kind of books she did.

One noteworthy thing I gathered from Geraldine was that her mother (highly academic as a young woman, even before she found her vocation in fiction) was invariably to be found immersed in her latest writing project – to the exclusion, at times, of her family. Geraldine also told me that her mother was notorious within the home for embroidering the truth, and was quite often caught out by her family for telling 'little white lies'. Geraldine, however, read no badness into this trait: she simply put it down to her mother's creative streak, her ability to fabricate new identities for people – even for herself.

Who, then, was the real Celia Fremlin? The short biographies in her books tended to state that she was born in Ryarsh, Kent. Geraldine, however, informed me that her mother was raised in Hertfordshire, where – we know for a fact – she was admitted to Berkhamsted School for Girls in 1923; she studied there until 1933. Ryarsh, then, was perhaps one of those minor fabrications on Fremlin's part. As a fan of hers, was I perturbed by the idea that Fremlin may have practised deceit? Not at all – if anything, it made the author and her works appear even more attractive and labyrinthine. Here was a middle-class woman who seemed to delight in re-inventing herself; and while all writers draw upon their own experiences to some extent, 'reinvention' is the key to any artist's longevity. I can imagine it must have been maddening to live with, but it does suggest Fremlin had a mischievous streak, evident too in her writing. And Fremlin is hardly alone in this habit, even among writers: haven't we all, at one time or another, 'embellished' some part of our lives to make us sound more interesting?

Even as a girl, Celia Fremlin wrote keenly: a talent perhaps inherited from her mother, Margaret, who had herself enjoyed writing plays. By the age of thirteen Celia was publishing poems in the *Chronicle of the Berkhamsted School for Girls*, and in 1930 she was awarded the school's

Lady Cooper Prize for 'Best Original Poem', her entry entitled, 'When the World Has Grown Cold' (which could easily have served for one of her later short stories). In her final year at Berkhamsted she became President of the school's inaugural Literary and Debating Society.

She went on to study Classics at Somerville College, Oxford, graduating with a second. Not one to rest on her laurels, she worked concurrently as a charwoman. This youthful experience provided a fascinating lesson for her in studying the class system from different perspectives, and led to her publishing her first non-fiction book, *The Seven Chars of Chelsea*, in 1940. During the war Fremlin served as an air-raid warden and also became involved in the now celebrated Mass Observation project of popular anthropology, founded in 1937 by Tom Harrisson, Charles Madge and Humphrey Jennings, and committed to the study of the everyday lives of ordinary people. Fremlin collaborated with Tom Harrisson on the book *War Factory* (1943), recording the experiences and attitudes of women war workers in a factory outside Malmesbury, Wiltshire, which specialised in making radar equipment.

In 1942, Fremlin married Elia Goller: they would have three children, Nicholas, Geraldine and Sylvia. According to Geraldine, the newlyweds moved to Hampstead, into a 'tall, old house overlooking the Heath itself', and this was where Geraldine and her siblings grew up. Fremlin was by now developing her fiction writing, and she submitted a number of short stories to the likes of *Women's Own*, *Punch* and the *London Mystery Magazine*. However she had to endure a fair number of rejections before, finally, her debut novel was accepted. In a preface to a later Pandora edition of said novel

PREFACE TO THE 2014 EDITION

Fremlin wrote:

> The original inspiration for this book was my second baby. She was one of those babies who, perfectly content and happy all day, simply don't sleep through the night. Soon after midnight she would wake; and again at half past two; and again at four. As the months went by, I found myself quite distracted by lack of sleep; my eyes would fall shut while I peeled the potatoes or ironed shirts. I remember one night sitting on the bottom step of the stairs, my baby awake and lively in my arms it dawned on me: this is a major human experience, why hasn't someone written about it? It seemed to me that a serious novel should be written with this experience at its centre. Then it occurred to me – why don't I write one?

The baby who bore unknowing witness to Fremlin's epiphany was, of course, Geraldine. It would be some years before Fremlin could actually put pen to paper on this project, but the resulting novel, *The Hours Before Dawn* (1959), went on to win the Edgar Award for Best Crime Novel from the Mystery Writers of America, and remains Fremlin's most famous work.

Thereafter Fremlin wrote at a steady pace, publishing *Uncle Paul* in 1960 and *Seven Lean Years* in 1961. Those first three novels have been classed as 'tales of menace', even 'domestic suspense'. Fremlin took the everyday as her subject and yet, by introducing an atmosphere of unease, she made it extraordinary, fraught with danger. She succeeded in chilling and thrilling her readers without spilling so much as a drop of blood. However, there is a persistent threat of harm that pervades Fremlin's writing and she excels at creating a claustrophobic tension in 'normal' households. This scenario was her métier and one she revisited in many novels. Fremlin once commented that her favourite pastimes were gossip, 'talking shop' and any kind of argument about anything. We might suppose that it was through these enthusiasms that she gleaned the ideas that grew into her books. Reading them it is clear that the mundane minutiae of domesticity fascinated her. Moreover, *The Hours Before Dawn* and *The Trouble-Makers* have a special concern with the societal/peer-group systems that adjudge whether or not a woman is rated a 'good wife' and 'good mother.'

*

By 1968 Celia Fremlin had established herself as a published author. But this was to be a year for the Goller family in which tragedy followed hard upon tragedy. Their youngest daughter Sylvia committed suicide, aged nineteen. A month later Fremlin's husband Elia killed himself. In the wake of these catastrophes Fremlin relocated to Geneva for a year.

In 1969 she published a novel entitled *Possession*. The manuscript had been delivered to Gollancz before the terrible events of 1968, but knowing of those circumstances in approaching *Possession* today makes for chilling reading, since incidents in the novel appear to mirror Fremlin's life at that time. It is one of her most absorbing and terrifying productions. Aside from the short-story collection *Don't Go to Sleep in the Dark* (1970) Fremlin did not publish again until *Appointment With Yesterday* (1972), subsequently a popular title amongst her body of work. The novel deals with a woman who has changed her identity: a recurrent theme, and one with which Fremlin may have identified most acutely in the aftermath of her terrible dual bereavements. *The Long Shadow* (1975) makes use of the knowledge of the Classics she acquired at Oxford; its main character, Imogen, is newly widowed. Again, we might suppose this was Fremlin's way of processing, through fictions, the trials she had suffered in her own life.

Fremlin lived on in Hampstead and married her second husband, Leslie Minchin, in 1985. The couple remained together until his death in 1999. She collaborated with Minchin on a book of poetry called *Duet in Verse* which appeared in 1996. Her last published novel was *King of the World* (1994). Geraldine believed that her mother's earlier work was her best, but I feel that this final novel, too, has its merits. Fremlin marvellously describes a woman who has been transformed from a dowdy, put-upon frump to an attractive woman of stature. The reason Fremlin gives for this seems to me revealing: 'Disaster itself, of course. However much a disaster sweeps away, it also inevitably leaves a slate clean.'

Though Geraldine did not admit as much to me, she did allude to having had a somewhat mixed relationship with her mother. This, in a way, explained to me the recurrence of the theme of mother–daughter relations explored in many of Fremlin's novels, from *Uncle Paul, Prisoner's Base* and *Possession* right up to her penultimate novel The Echoing Stones (1993). One wonders whether Fremlin hoped that the fictional exploration of this theme might help her to attain a better understanding of it in life. Thankfully, as they got older and Celia moved to Bristol to be nearer Geraldine, both women managed finally to find some common ground and discovered a mutual respect for each other. Celia Fremlin was, in the end, pre-deceased by all three of her children. She died herself in 2009.

To revisit the Celia Fremlin *oeuvre* now is to see authentic snapshots of how people lived at the time of her writing: how they interacted, what values they held. Note how finely Fremlin denotes the relations between child and adult, husband and wife, woman and woman. Every interaction between her characters has a core of truth and should strike a resonant note in any reader. Look carefully for the minute gestures that can have devastating consequences. Watch as the four walls of your comforting home can be turned into walls of a prison. Above all, enjoy feeling unsettled as Fremlin's words push down on you, making you feel just as claustrophobic as her characters as they confront their fates. Fremlin was a superb writer who has always enjoyed a core of diehard fans and yet, despite her Edgar Award success, was not to achieve the readership she deserved. As Faber Finds now reissue her complete works, now is the time to correct that.

*

Celia Fremlin's short stories, of which she published three collections in her writing career, are superbly constructed. In only a few pages she is able to convey that desperate feeling of unease worthy of any of her full-length novels. But the short form seemed to give Fremlin special licence to throw caution to the wind, and the tales collected in *Don't Go to Sleep in the Dark* serve up a selection of eclectic, delectable, perfectly formed nibbles. Fremlin's familiar theme of strained mother–child relations is explored in 'The Baby Sitter' and the chilling 'The Hated House'. However, here she delves into the supernatural realm as well as the psychological.

Another theme that seemed to fascinate and frighten Fremlin was ageing. She was moving into her late fifties as this collection was published, and the concerns of old age are discernible in some of the stories. Fremlin is careful to give her elderly characters distinctive voices, also articulating their sense of frustration and injustice very succinctly in 'Old Daniel's Treasure' and 'Last Day of Spring', making them fully three-dimensional. But Fremlin was also adept at deceiving the reader, often by way of playing on the self-deceiving tendencies of her characters, and she uses this device with skill here, too. It's important to note how often Fremlin manages to add dashes of sly humour, exhibited perfectly in 'The Betrayal', 'For Ever Fair' and 'The Fated Interview'. One can easily imagine that as she wrote each of these small gems she had her tongue firmly planted in her cheek.

Don't Go to Sleep in the Dark is a wonderful collection that showcases Fremlin's array of talents to great effect. The short form is much less fashionable today, but Fremlin deployed it expertly to deliver delicate and bittersweet bite-sized slices of life.

Chris Simmons
www.crimesquad.com

THE QUIET GAME

IT WAS NOT Hilda who first talked of being driven mad, up there in the high flats, far above the noise of the traffic and the bustle of the crowds. On the contrary, it was her neighbours who complained to *her* about the stresses. "It's driving me up the wall!" said her neighbour on the right: and "I can't stand it any longer!" said her neighbour on the left: and "I'll go out of my mind!" said the woman in the flat below. But not Hilda. Hilda was the young one, the busy one. From the point of view of the neighbours it was she who was the cause and origin of all the stresses. *She* wasn't the one who was being driven mad, Oh no. That's what they would all have told you.

But madness has a rhythm of its own up there so near to the clouds; a rhythm that at first you would not recognize, so near is it, in the beginning, to the rhythms of ordinary, cheerful life...

"What's the *time*, Mr Wolf? What's the *time*, Mr Wolf?" Thumpty-*thump*-thump-thump. Thumpty-*thump*-thump-thump ... The twins' shrill little voices, the thud of their firm little sandalled feet reverberated through the door of the kitchenette and brought Hilda to a sudden halt in the midst of the morning's wash. Her arms elbow-deep in warm detergent, she just stood there, while the familiar, helpless anger rose slowly from the pit of her stomach. She would have to stop them, of course; the innocent, happy little game would have to be brought once more to a halt by yet another "No!" And quickly too, before Mrs Walters in the flat below came up to protest; before Mr Peters on the right tapped on the wall; before Miss Rice on the left leaned across the balcony to complain of her head and to tell Hilda how well children were brought up in *her* young days.

Miss Rice's young days were all very well; in those days children had space for play and romping. If they were rich they had fields and lawns and nurseries and schoolrooms; if they were poor, they had at least the streets and the alley ways. But today's children, the sky-dwellers of the affluent twentieth century, where could *they* go to run, to shout, to fulfil their childhood? All day long, up here in the blue emptiness of the sky, Hilda had to deprive her children, minute by minute, of everything that matters in childhood. They must not run, or jump, or laugh, or sing, or dance. They must not play hide-and-seek or cowboys and Indians, or fling themselves with shrieks of joy into piles of cushions. Except when she could find time to take them to the distant park, they must sit still, like chronic invalids, growing dull and pale over television and picture books.

"What's the *time*, Mr Wolf? ... One o'clock—two o'clock three o'clock...." Thumpty-*thump*-thump-thump.

Hilda had a vision of the sturdy little thighs in identical navy shorts, stamping purposefully round and round the room, little faces alight with the intoxication of rhythm and with the mounting excitement of the approaching climax. Before this climax—before the wild shriek of "*Dinner*-time, Mr Wolf!" rent the silence of the flats, Hilda would have to go in and spoil it all. "Martin! Sally!" she would have to say, "You really must be quieter. Why don't you get out your colouring books, and come and sit quietly? Come along, now, over here at the table." And she would have to watch the bright little faces grow tearful, hear the merry, chanting voices take on the whine of boredom; watch the firm, taut little muscles relinquish their needed exercise and grow flaccid as they sat ... and sat ... and sat. It was wicked, it was cruel....

"Mrs Meredith? Could I speak to you for a minute, Mrs Meredith?"

So. Already she had left it too late. Here was Miss Rice out on her balcony, hand on brow, headache poised like a weapon, and already sure of her victory.

"It's not that I want to complain," she began, as she began every morning "And if it was just for myself, I suppose I'd try to put up with it, but it's Mrs Walters too, she hasn't been too well either, and it's driving her up the wall, it really is, all this hammer, hammer, hammer. She's just phoned through to me, asked if I could have a word with you, save her coming up the stairs with her bad knee."

Bad knees. Headaches. Not-too-well-ness. These were the weapons by which happy little four-year-olds could be crushed and broken; there was no defence against them.

"I'm sorry," said Hilda despairingly; and again "I'm sorry ... I'm sorry...."

The twins had been settled at their colouring books for nearly an hour before Mrs Walters below rang up to enquire if Hilda couldn't somehow stop that boom-boom noise? "Boom-boom-*boom*" the clipped voice mimicked explanatorily down the wire. "It goes right through my nerves, Mrs Meredith, it really does. I can't think what they can be doing, little kiddies like that, I can't think what they can be *doing*."

Firing cannon? Riding roller-coasters round the room? No, it turned out to be Sally's energetic rubbing-out of her drawing of a cat. It wobbled the table, it set the floor vibrating.

"No, Sally, don't use the rubber any more, just colour it how it is, there's a good girl."

"No, Martin, you must keep your dinky-car on the rug, Mrs Walters will hear it on the linoleum."

"No, Sally, leave that chair where it is, we don't want Mr Peters knocking on the wall again."

No.... No.... No. Two lively little creatures reduced to tears and tempers, to sobbing, hopeless boredom.

Nevertheless, it wasn't Hilda saying "I can't stand it!" It was Miss Rice. And Mr Peters. And Mrs Walters.

Autumn passed into winter, and it was less and less often possible to take the twins to the park. Their bounding morning spirits had to be crushed earlier and earlier in the day. The search for a quiet game, for something that wouldn't annoy the neighbours, became a day-long preoccupation for Hilda; but in spite of all her efforts nothing, nothing seemed quiet enough; for still, without respite, came the voices, from above, below, on every side:

"Really, Mrs Meredith, if you *could* keep them a little quieter...."

"Mrs Meredith, I don't want to seem to complain, but...."

"Mrs Meredith, sometimes I think it's a herd of elephants you've got up there...."

"It's not that I don't love kiddies, Mrs Meredith, but that's not the same as letting them grow up little hooligans, is it, Mrs Meredith?"

"It's my head, Mrs Meredith."

"It's my nerves, Mrs Meredith."

"I've not been feeling too well, Mrs Meredith."

So No, No, No, all through the grey November days. No, Martin. Stop it, Sally. *No*. No! No! No! The twins grew whiney and quarrelsome; their sturdy little legs looked thinner, their faces paler.

And still it wasn't Hilda who said "I can't stand it." It was Miss Rice. And Mr Peters. And Mrs Walters.

It was the new carpet that gave her the idea; the new square of carpet bought to deaden the sound of footsteps in the hallway. It was not really new, it was second-hand and somewhat worn, but the twins were enchanted by it. They had never seen a Persian carpet before, and for a whole afternoon there was silence so absolute that not a word of complaint came from above or from below or from either side. From lunch-time till dusk, Martin and

Sally crouched on the carpet examining every brown and crimson flower, every purple scroll and every pinkish coil of leaves. Hilda felt quite light-headed with happiness; a whole afternoon with the twins truly enjoying themselves and the neighbours not complaining!

"It's a *magic* carpet!" she told them hopefully, when she saw that their interest was beginning to flag. "Why don't you sit on it and shut your eyes, and it'll take you to wonderful places. See? Off it goes! You're flying off above the rooftops now, you're looking down, and you can see all the houses, and the streets, and the trains...."

"And the Zoo!" chimed in Sally. "I can see the Zoo and all the animals in it. I can see the tigers and the lions..."

"And now we're over the sea!" squealed Martin. "I can see the whales and the submarines and—and—Oh, look! Look, Sally, I can see an island! Let's stop at that island, let's go and live there!"

The game took hold. The perfect quiet game had been found at last. Hour after hour the twins would sit on the carpet travelling from land to land, and seeing strange and wonderful sights as they went. They would land in Siberia, or at the South Pole, or on a South Sea Island, where wild adventures would befall them, and they only escaped in time to fly home in time for tea.

But their favourite destination of all was Inkoo Land. In Inkoo Land there were tiny elephants just big enough to ride on; there were twisty, knobbly trees, wonderful for climbing, and from which you could pick all the kinds of fruit in the world. There were wide spaces of grass to run on, there was a jungle to play hide-and-seek in, there were monkeys who talked monkey-language, and Sally and Martin learned it too, with fantastic speed and ease; and then they played with the monkeys, swinging from branch to branch through the green, sun-spangled forests.

But always, in the end, they had to come home; they grew tired of sitting even on a *magic* carpet; and the moment they disembarked and set foot on the floor, the voices would start again, from all around:

"It's my head, Mrs Meredith."

"It's my nerves, Mrs Meredith."

"It's not what I'm used to, Mrs Meredith, it's making me ill, it really is!"

If only they could stay in Inkoo Land all day! Such a lovely game it was—there were moments when Hilda caught herself thinking how good it was for them, on the grey winter afternoons, to have all that exercise, rushing through the sunny glades, and clambering about in the forest trees. So much better for them than the steely winter park, with its asphalt paths and "Keep Off the Grass" notices.

Then she would recollect herself, smile a little wryly at her own childishness in getting so caught up in her children's fantasies, and set herself to preparing tea ready for their "return".

But at last, inevitably, the novelty of the game began to wear off: the "return" became earlier and earlier; and one day, a grey, hopeless day of fog and cold, the twins refused to go to Inkoo Land at all.

Hilda was conscious of a sickening, overmastering despair. They *must* go to Inkoo Land! In vain she pleaded, bribed, even scolded. Go to Inkoo Land they would not.

"We've got nothing to *do*, Mummy." the old cry began again; and as if at a pre-arranged signal the voices returned, above, below and all around:

"It's my nerves, Mrs Meredith."

"It's my head, Mrs Meredith."

"I don't want to complain, Mrs Meredith."

"The doctor says I need rest, Mrs Meredith."

The voices seemed to go on and on, whispering in the air, sighing in through the window, seeping in under the doors, and suddenly Hilda knew what she must do.

"*I'll* come with you to Inkoo Land," she declared. "You must show it to me—I've never seen it, you know."

The twins interest was at once revived; they scrambled eagerly on to the carpet. "Mummy come too! Mummy come too!" they chanted; and when they were all seated on the carpet, Martin gave his orders in a clear little treble. "Inkoo Land, please!" he told the carpet; and they all clutched each other tight against the tipping and rocking to be expected as the carpet lifted itself off the floor.

But what had gone wrong? The carpet didn't move at all! Hilda stared stupidly round the four walls that still enclosed them.

"Say it again, Martin!" she urged him; and, a little surprised, the child obeyed.

Still nothing happened. Hilda felt her heart beating strangely. Was it too heavy for the carpet, having to carry an adult as well as the two children? Or—why, that was it!—they should be near a window! How could they expect the carpet to fly if there was no window to fly out of? Jumping up, she hurried into the living room and opened the window wide to the foggy winter air.

"Bring the carpet in here!" she called, and hurried out to help the twins drag it in from the hall.

She was surprised to see them both looking a little frightened. Sally's lips were quivering. "Play properly, Mummy!" she pleaded: and: "Oooo—it's *cold* in here!" complained Martin, as they laid out the carpet in the sitting room, now slowly filling with swirls of icy fog.

"Never mind. We'll soon be in Inkoo Land," Hilda encouraged them. "On to the carpet, both of you. We'll soon be in the lovely warm forest now, with the sun shining, and all the monkeys and the elephants. Say the words, Martin; say them again."

And *still* the carpet didn't move. The three of them together must definitely be too heavy, decided Hilda; they would have to help the carpet. One could see how hard it must be to lift the whole lot of them bodily off the floor; but if they were to give it a start by launching it off the window sill, then it would be able to glide along easily above the roof tops.

But why were the twins crying? Backing, hand in hand, away from the window, refusing to help as she dragged the unwieldy thing on to the ledge of the open window?

What a floppy sort of magic carpet it was! How it hung, limply, half in and half out of the window, dangling down on either side! But of course it would stiffen up when it began to fly. She clambered awkwardly on to the ledge and sat herself, as well as she could, balancing, on the carpet-covered sill. She began to feel excited. In a minute now she would be in Inkoo Land. Instead of this chilling fog, there would be a tropic sun beating down upon her; leaves on the great trees would shimmer in the golden light; bright tropical flowers would be there, and luxuriant creepers; and she would see her little twins romping joyously at last: running, shouting, jumping in the sunshine, far, far from the complaining voices.

"*Mrs Meredith!*" came, for one last time, the shocked voice of Miss Rice on her balcony; but already it seemed far, far away, a little thread of sound from the world of fog and chill which Hilda was leaving. "To Inkoo Land!" she cried to the carpet, and together they launched forth from the High Flats into the swirling, silver emptiness of the sky.

It was warm in Inkoo Land, just as she had known it would be; and there was grass, and great forest trees, and the sun shone. The grass was like great sweeps of lawn, and once or twice the twins had come, to run about on it, and laugh, and shout, and turn head over heels, just as she had imagined. But mostly it was people like herself, wandering slowly among the trees; and other people, in white coats, moving more briskly. And several times Miss Rice had mysteriously appeared, a quite changed Miss Rice, crying, and saying, "If only we had known!" and "When you come back, dear, everything will be different." Miss Rice, it seemed, had saved her "in the nick of time"; but somehow Hilda couldn't think about that just yet, not about the long, long problem that lay behind. Enough, for the moment, to be in Inkoo Land, and to know that, sooner or later, she would return, just as the twins had always returned, in time for tea.

THE BETRAYAL

MAISIE WALTER'S LIPS stretched in a tight little smile of satisfaction as she surveyed the poky suburban house with its prim lace curtains. So *this* was what Mark had come to, after thirty years! Mark, with his gay, defiant opinions, his much-vaunted scorn of convention—the god-like Mark had come to this in the end!

It was the end, of course. The unspecified female relative who had written to Julia in a crabbed and elderly hand had made that perfectly clear, in spite of the circumlocutions in which such a statement must decently be couched. Mark had at most a few more months to live, and he wanted to see his old friend Maisie Walter before he died; that was the gist of the letter which Maisie now fingered almost lovingly with her tight black glove.

The triumph of it! Mark, who had once thought that he owned the world—that he owned Maisie, and could demand of her anything he liked—Mark now lay dying in this genteel-ly squalid street, with only some ageing cousin or something to look after him. Not even a wife or family to show for all that proud young strength! A little secret smile hovered round Maisie's mouth, and she rang the bell.

The female relative had retired, still dimly chattering, down the dim linoleumed stairs, and Maisie was left to enter the bedroom alone. She hesitated—not from any fear of what she might feel at the sight of her lover, alone and dying, after thirty years, but from some uncertainty as to whether or not to keep on her hat and gloves. Both were becoming—the hat, in particular, with its crisp little veil, was a valuable addition to the ever more complicated apparatus necessary for making people exclaim that she didn't look a day over forty. The gloves too— everyone knows that well-chosen gloves can do a lot for a woman past her first girlhood. On the other hand, it would be nice for him to notice, as he lay there with his once all-dominating, all-demanding body ruined and shrunken, that *her* hair was still yellow and shining; that *her* hands were still white, and beautifully manicured. She couldn't actually *show* him her luxurious house in Richmond, or her prosperous stockbroker husband, but she'd soon get them into the conversation.

"Maisie?"

The voice from the bed did not sound either broken or humble, and Maisie was momentarily irritated and taken aback. Then she recovered herself, cautiously made her face light up with the smile which showed her top teeth but not her less natural-looking bottom ones, and approached the bed. Her confidence flowed warmly back at the sight of the gaunt figure leaning against the pillows. The looks were gone; the fire was gone; the blue eyes whose glance had once made her forget everything else on earth—well, not quite everything, thank goodness, or she wouldn't now be living in that comfortable house in Richmond—those eyes had faded to a lustreless, bloodshot grey.

"How are you, Mark?" she enquired brightly, and added: "I've brought you some flowers."

She dumped the twelve red roses on to the bed. Something cheaper would have done, but she had only remembered at the last minute that one is supposed to bring an invalid something and roses were all she could see to buy.

She waited for him to thank her—to look her up and down and tell her she looked as beautiful as ever—to ask her how she was getting on—all the remarks one has a right to expect in such a situation. But he didn't say any of these things. He simply gazed at the flowers lying on the blanket in front of him, as if in deep thought. Suddenly he spoke, with a curious flash of the old arrogance—an arrogance that had no right to survive in so changed a body.

"Let me see your hands, Maisie. I haven't seen your hands for thirty years."

Startled, Maisie removed her gloves and held out her hands, palms downwards so that the perfectly varnished nails would show to best advantage. Sharply, he turned them over and looked at the palms.

"Why, Maisie!" he said, in tones of gentle surprise. "They're still beautiful!"

He looked up at her in a sort of bewilderment, and Maisie bristled with annoyance. Still beautiful, indeed!

And why shouldn't they be, she'd like to know? Anybody else would have told her that *she* still looked beautiful... not a day over forty....

She forced a smile back on to her face—the condescending one this time. He must be made to realize how completely the tables were turned since last they were together.

"Shall I put the flowers in water for you?" she enquired briskly.

"*Yes!* Oh, yes, *please!*" he said, with a vehemence that made her start; "And when you've done that," he went on, with a strange, tense eagerness, "I'm going to ask you to do something else for me."

As Maisie poked the roses one after another into the hideous glass vase produced by the relative from some dank cupboard downstairs, she was conscious of Mark's eyes on her all the time. No, not on *her*—on her hands; and she flashed her diamonds and nail varnish as well as she could without actually pricking herself on those beastly stalks.

"Do you remember, Maisie, the last time I watched you arranging red roses in a vase?"

He spoke slowly with his eyes on her hands as if he were asking them the question rather than her. "Red roses. I'd brought them to you. It was the most beautiful sight I had ever seen—your hands moving among the flowers." He stopped. "I asked you for something then, Maisie, which you never gave me. Now I am going to ask you for something else—something which you may find it easier to give."

Maisie eyed him guardedly, and he went on: "I just

want you to get me the bottle of sleeping tablets from the bathroom. The doctor won't let me have them within reach—nor will Cousin Edie. Mine is a painful complaint, you know," he added gently, "and there is no one else I can ask to help me. I promise you nothing will happen till you are safe home again. No one will be able to blame you. Please, Maisie, just get them for me. It won't take you a moment. In remembrance of the roses, all those years ago."

Maisie stared at him, scandalized. Was there no limit to the outrageous demands this man would make on her? Once it had been demands that no respectable girl could submit to, and now it was this! Expecting her to abet him in an actual *crime*!

She drew herself up—and then faltered. If she refused point blank there would be a scene, and she had long ago had enough scenes with Mark to last her a lifetime. Better humour him—pretend she couldn't find them, or something.... With face averted she hurried off and found the bathroom.

A fine array of bottles there, and no mistake. Cousin Edie must have almost as many things the matter with her as Mark himself! But she saw the bottle Mark meant—two of them, in fact—one nearly full, the other empty.

It was the empty one that gave her the idea—the clever, amusing idea that would get her so neatly out of the whole business. All she had to do was fill it with tablets that looked similar but were really harmless—in all this collection there must be something that would do. Then she could take it to Mark, and he'd never know the difference until—well, until *she* was safely out of the house!

Ah! The very thing! Vitamin tablets! They looked almost the same, and one could take dozens of them and come to no harm! Giggling like a schoolgirl, she tipped a number of them into the empty bottle, touched up her make-up in the bathroom mirror, and then, scarcely able to keep a straight face, she returned to the bedroom.

How his face lit up! Maisie could have giggled aloud as he snatched the bottle from her like a starving man and stuffed it under his pillow; as he kissed her white hand over and over again, with tears of gratitude in his eyes.

"You must go now, my love, my darling!" he cried, in a choked voice. "You must get right away from this house, safe home again, before I take them. And listen, Maisie. All the days of your life my blessing will follow you. Wherever my soul may be in all this wide universe, it will never forget what you have risked, what you have done for me today. Tonight, as the last, blessed drowsiness steals over me, I shall lie here looking at your roses, thinking of your white hands. They shall be my last thought—the brave and lovely hands that have given me my release...."

Really, it seemed as if he'd never get to the end of his speech. Maisie almost had to stuff her handkerchief into her mouth to keep from laughing outright. Honestly, it was killing! To think of him lying here tonight, gazing soulfully at red roses and lapping up vitamin tablets! Once she was safe outside in the street, Maisie stood and laughed until her sides ached.

It wasn't until the next day, when she heard that Mark

Wilkinson had died in the night from an overdose of sleeping tablets, that she realized the silly mistake she must have made. She'd just put the bottle down for a moment while she touched up her face, and then in her hurry she must have picked up the wrong one and given it to him. Maddening! Such a clever trick it would have been. How was it that her hands, her beautiful hands, should have so betrayed her?

THE NEW HOUSE

Looking back, I find it hard to say just when it was that I first began to feel anxious about my niece, Linda. No—anxious is not quite the right word, for of course I have been anxious about her many times during the ten years she has been in my care. You see, she has never been a robust girl, and when she first came to live with me, a nervous, delicate child of twelve, she seemed so frail that I really wondered sometimes if she would survive to grow up. However, I am happy to say that she grew stronger as the years passed, and I flatter myself that by gentle, common-sense handling and abundant affection I have turned her into as strong and healthy a young woman as she could ever have hoped to be. Stronger, I am sure, (though perhaps I shouldn't say this) than she would have been if my poor sister had lived to bring her up.

No, it was not anxiety about Linda's health that had troubled me during the past weeks; nor was it simply a natural anxiety about the wisdom of her engagement to John Barlow. He seemed a pleasant enough young man, with his freckled, snub-nosed face and ginger hair. Though I have to admit I didn't really take to him myself—he

THE NEW HOUSE

made me uneasy in some way I can't describe. But I would not dream of allowing this queer prejudice of mine to stand in the way of the young couple—there is nothing I detest more than this sort of interference by the older generation.

All the same, I must face the fact that it was only after I heard of their engagement that I began to experience any qualms of fear about Linda—those first tremors of a fear that was to grow and grow until it became an icy terror that never left me, day or night.

I think it was in September that I first became aware of my uneasiness—a gusty September evening with autumn in the wind—in the trees—everywhere. I was cycling up the long gentle hill from the village after a particularly wearisome and inconclusive committee meeting of the Women's Institute. I was tired—so tired that before I reached the turning into our lane I found myself getting off my bicycle to push it up the remainder of the slope— a thing I have never done before. For in spite of my fifty-four years I am a strong woman, and a busy one. I cycle everywhere, in all weathers, and it is rare indeed for me to feel tired, certainly the gentle incline between the village and our house had never troubled me before. But tonight, somehow, the bicycle might have been made of lead—I felt as if I had cycled fifteen miles instead of the bare one and a half from the village; and when I turned into the dripping lane, and the evening became almost night under the overhanging trees, I became aware not only of tiredness, but of an indefinable foreboding. The dampness and the autumn dusk seemed to have crept into my very soul, bringing their darkness with them.

Well, I am not a fanciful woman. I soon pulled myself together when I reached home, switched on the lights, and made myself a cup of tea. Strong and sweet it was, the way I always like it. Linda often laughs at me about my tea—she likes hers so thin and weak that I sometimes wonder why she bothers to pour the water into the teapot at all, instead of straight from the kettle to her cup!

So there I sat, the comfortable old kitchen chair drawn up to the glowing stove, and I waited for the warmth and the sweet tea to work their familiar magic. But somehow, this evening, they failed. Perhaps I was really *too* tired; or perhaps it was the annoyance of noticing from the kitchen clock that it was already after eight. As I have told you, I am a busy woman, and to find that that tiresome meeting must have taken a good two hours longer than usual *was* provoking, especially as I had planned to spend a good long evening working on the Girls' Brigade accounts.

Whatever it may have been, somehow I couldn't relax. The stove crackled merrily; the tea was delicious; yet still I sat, tense and uneasy, as if waiting for something.

And then, somehow, I must have gone to sleep, quite suddenly; because the next thing I knew I was dreaming. Quite a simple, ordinary sort of dream it will seem to you—nothing alarming, nothing even unusual in it, and yet you will have to take my word for it that it had all the quality of a nightmare.

I dreamed that I was watching Linda at work in the new house. I should explain here that for the past few months Linda has not been living here with me, but in lodgings in the little town where she works, about six

THE NEW HOUSE

miles from here. It is easier for her getting to and from the office, and also it means that she and John can spend their evenings working at the new house they have been lucky enough to get in the Estate on the outskirts of the town. It is not quite finished yet, and they are doing all the decorations themselves—I believe John is putting up shelves and cupboards and all kinds of clever fittings. I am telling you this so that you will see that there was nothing intrinsically nightmarish about the setting of my dream—on the contrary, the little place must have been full of happiness and bustling activity—the most unlikely background for a nightmare that you could possibly imagine.

Well, in my dream I was there with them. Not with them in any active sense, you understand, but hovering in that disembodied way one does in dreams—an observer, not an actor in the scene. Somewhere near the top of the stairs I seemed to be, and looking down I could see Linda through the door of one of the empty little rooms. It was late afternoon in my dream, and the pale rainy light gleamed on her flaxen-pale hair making it look almost metallic—a sort of shining grey. She had her back to me, and she seemed absorbed in distempering the far wall of the room—I seemed to hear that sucksucking noise of the distemper brush with extraordinary vividness.

And as I watched her, I began to feel afraid. She looked so tiny, and thin, and unprotected; her fair, childlike head seemed poised somehow so precariously on her white neck—even her absorption in the painting seemed in my dream to add somehow to her peril. I opened my mouth to warn her—of I know not what—but I could make no sound, as is the way of dreams. It was then that the whole thing slipped into nightmare. I tried to scream—to run—I struggled in vain to wake up—and as the nightmare mounted I became aware of footsteps, coming nearer and nearer through the empty house. "It's only John!" I told myself in the dream, but even as the words formed themselves in my brain, I knew I had touched the very core of my terror. This man whose every glance and movement had always filled me with uneasiness—already the light from some upstairs room was casting his shadow, huge and hideous, across the landing.... I struggled like a thing demented to break the paralysis of nightmare. And then, somehow, I was running, running, running....

I woke up, sick and shaking, the sweat pouring down my face. For a moment I thought a great hammering on the door had woken me, but then I realized that it was only the beating of my heart, thundering and pounding so that it seemed to shake the room.

Well, I have told you before that I am a strong woman, not given to nerves and fancies. Linda is the one who suffers from that sort of thing, not me. Time and again in her childhood I had to go to her in the night and soothe her off to sleep again after some wild dream. But for *me*, a grown woman, who never in her life has feared or run away from anything—for *me* to wake up weak and shaking like a baby from a childish nightmare! I shook it off angrily, got out of my chair and fetched my papers, and, as far as I can remember, worked on the Girls' Brigade accounts far into the night.

THE NEW HOUSE

I thought no more about it until, perhaps a week or so later, the same thing happened again. The same sort of rainy evening, the same coming home quite unusually tired—and then the same dream. Well, not quite the same. This time Linda wasn't distempering; she was on hands and knees—staining the floor or something of the sort. And there were no footsteps. This time nothing happened at all; only there was a sense of evil, of brooding hatred, which seemed to fill the little house. Somehow I felt it to be focussed on the little figure kneeling in its gaily-patterned overall. The hatred seemed to thicken round her—I could feel giant waves of it converging on her, mounting silently, silkily till they hung poised above her head in ghastly, silent strength. Again I tried to scream a warning; again no sound came; and again I woke, weak and trembling, in my chair.

This time I was really worried. The tie between me and Linda is very close—closer, I think, than the tie between her and her mother could ever have been. Common-sense sort of person though I am, I could not help wondering whether these dreams were not some kind of warning. Should I ring her up, and ask if everything was all right? I scolded myself for the very idea! I mustn't give way to such foolish, hysterical fancies—I have always prided myself on letting Linda lead her own life, and not smothering her with possessive anxiety as her mother would have done. Stop! I mustn't keep speaking of Linda's mother like this—of Angela—of my own sister. Angela has been dead many years now, and whatever wrong I may have suffered from her once has all been forgotten and forgiven years ago—I am not a woman to harbour grievances. But, of course, all this business of Linda's approaching marriage was bound to bring it back to me in a way. I couldn't help remembering that I, too, was once preparing a little house ready for my marriage; that Richard once looked into my eyes just as John now looks into Linda's.

Well, I suppose most old maids have some ancient—and usually boring—love story hidden somewhere in their pasts, and I don't think mine will interest you much—it doesn't even interest me after all these years, so I will tell it as briefly as I can.

When I fell in love with Richard I was already twenty-eight, tall and angular, and a school-teacher into the bargain. So it seemed to me like a miracle that he, so handsome, gay and charming should love me in return and ask me to marry him. Our only difficulty was that my parents were both dead, and I was the sole support of my young sister, Angela. We talked it over, and decided to wait a year, until Angela had left school and could support herself.

But at the end of the year it appeared that Angela had set her heart on a musical career. Tearfully she begged me to see her through her first two years at college; after that, she was sure she could fend for herself.

Well, Richard was difficult this time, and I suppose one can hardly blame him. He accused me of caring more for my sister than for him, of making myself a doormat, and much else that I forget. But at last it was agreed to wait for the two years, and meantime to work and save for a home together.

And work and save we did. By the end of the two years we had bought a little house, and we spent our evenings decorating and putting finishing touches to it, just as Linda and John are doing now.

Then came another blow. Angela failed in her exams. Again I was caught up in the old conflict; Richard angry and obstinate, Angela tearful and beseeching me to give her one more chance, for only six months this time. Once again I agreed, stipulating that this time was really to be the last. To my surprise, after his first outburst, Richard became quite reasonable about it; and soon after that he was sent away on a series of business trips, so that we saw much less of each other.

Then, one afternoon at the end of May, not long before the six months were up, something happened. I was sitting on the lawn correcting exercises when Angela came out of the house and walked slowly towards me. I remember noticing how sweetly pretty she looked with her flaxen hair and big blue eyes—just like Linda's now. The spring sunshine seemed to light up the delicacy of her too-pale skin, making it seem rare and lovely. She sat down on the grass beside me without speaking, and something in her silence made me lay down my pen.

"What is it, Angela?" I said. "Is anything the matter?"

She looked up at me then, her blue eyes full of childish defiance, and a sort of pride.

"Yes," she said. "I'm going to have a baby." She paused, looking me full in the face. "Richard's baby."

I didn't say anything. I don't even remember feeling anything. Even then, I suppose, I was a strong-minded person who did not allow her feelings to run away with her. Angela was still talking:

"And it's no use blaming *us*, Madge." She was saying. "What do you expect, after you've kept him dangling all these years?"

I remember the exercise book open in front of me, dazzling white in the May sunshine. One of the children had written "Nappoleon"—like that, with two p's—over and over again in her essay. There must have been half a dozen of them just on the one page. I felt I would go mad if I had to go on looking at them, so I took my pen and crossed them out, one after another, in red ink. Even to this day I have a foolish feeling that I would still go mad if I ever saw "Nappoleon" spelt like that again.

I felt as if a long time had passed, and Angela must have got up and gone away ages ago; but no, here she was, still talking:

"Well, *you* may not care, Madge," she was saying; "I don't suppose you'd stop correcting your old exercises if the world blew up. But what about *me*? What am I to *do*?"

I simply had to cross out the last of the "Nappoleon's" before I spoke.

"Do?" I said gently, "Why, Richard must marry you, of course. I'll talk to him myself."

Well, they were married, and Linda was born, a delicate, sickly little thing, weighing barely five pounds. Angela, too, was poorly. She had been terribly nervous and ill during her pregnancy and took a long time to recover; and it was tacitly agreed that there should be no more children. A pity, because I know Richard would have liked a large family. Strange how I, a strong healthy woman who could have raised half a dozen children without turning a hair, should have been denied the chance, while poor, sickly Angela ... Ah well, that is life. And I suppose my maternal feelings were largely satisfied by caring for poor delicate little Linda—it seemed only natural that when first her father and then Angela died the little orphan should come and live with me. And indeed I loved her dearly. She was my poor sister's child as well as Richard's, and my only fear has been that I may love her too deeply, too possessively, and so cramp her freedom.

Perhaps this fear is unfounded. Anyway, it was this that prevented me lifting the telephone receiver then and there on that rainy September night, dialling her number, and asking if all was well. If I had done so, would it have made any difference to what followed? Could I have checked the march of tragedy, then and there, when I woke from that second dream? I didn't know. I still don't know. All I know is that as I sat there in the silent room, listening to the rain beating against my windows out of the night, my fears somehow became clearer—came to a focus, as it were. I knew now, with absolute certainty, that what I feared had something to do with Linda's forthcoming marriage. Her marriage to John Barlow.

But what could it be? What *could* I be afraid of? He was such a pleasant, ordinary young man, from a respected local family; he had a good job; he loved Linda deeply. Well, he seemed to do so. And yet, as I thought about it, as I remembered the uneasiness I always felt in his presence, it occurred to me that this uneasiness—this anxiety for Linda's safety—was always at its height when he made some gesture of affection towards her—a light caress, perhaps—a quick, intimate glance across a crowded room....

Common sense. Common sense has been my ally throughout life, and I called in its aid now.

"There is nothing wrong!" I said aloud into the empty room; "There is nothing wrong with this young man!"

And then I went to bed.

It must have been nearly three weeks later when I had the dream again. I had seen Linda in the interval, and she seemed as well and happy as I have ever known her. The only cloud on her horizon was that for the next fortnight John would be working late, and so they wouldn't be able to spend the evenings painting and carpentering together in the new house.

"But I'll go on by myself, Auntie," she assured me; "I want to start on the woodwork in that front room tonight. Pale green, we thought, to go with the pink...." So she chattered on, happily and gaily, seeming to make nonsense of my fears.

"It sounds lovely, dear," I said; "Don't knock yourself up, though, working too hard."

For Linda *does* get tired easily. In spite of the thirty years difference in our age, I can always outpace her on our long rambles over the hills and arrive home fresh and vigorous while she is sometimes quite white with exhaustion.

"No, Auntie, don't worry," she said, standing on tiptoe to kiss me—she is such a little thing—"I won't get tired.

THE NEW HOUSE

I'm so happy, I don't think I'll ever get tired again!"

Reassuring enough, you'd have thought. And yet, somehow, it didn't reassure me. Her very happiness—even the irrelevant fact that John would be working late— seemed somehow to add to the intangible peril I could feel gathering round her.

And three nights later I dreamed the dream again.

This time, she was alone in the little house. I don't know how I knew it with such certainty in the dream, but I did—her aloneness seemed to fill the unfurnished rooms with echoes. *She* seemed nervous, too. She was no longer painting with the absorbed concentration of my previous dreams, but jerkily, uncertainly. She kept starting —turning round—listening; and I, hovering somewhere on the stairs as before, seemed to be listening too. Listening for what? For the fear which I knew was creeping like fog into the little house—or for something more?

"It's a dream!" I tried to cry, with soundless lips. "Don't be afraid, Linda, it's only a dream! I've had it before, I'll wake up soon! It's all right, I'm waking right now, I can hear the banging...."

I started awake in my chair, bolt upright, deafened by the now familiar thumping of my heart.

But was it my heart? Could that imperious knocking, which shook the house, be merely my heart? The knocking became interspersed with a frantic ringing of the bell. This was no dream. I staggered to my feet, and somehow got down the passage to the front door, and flung it open. There in the rainy night was Linda, Linda wild and white and dishevelled, flinging herself into my arms.

"Oh, Auntie, Auntie, I thought you were out—asleep —I couldn't make you hear—I rang and rang...."

I soothed her as best I could. I took her into the kitchen and made her a cup of the weak thin tea she loves, and heard her story.

And after all it wasn't much of a story. Just that she had gone to the new house as usual after work, and had settled down to painting the front room. For a while, she said, she had worked quite happily; and then suddenly she had heard a sound— a shuffling sound, so faint that she might almost have imagined it.

"And that was all, really, Auntie," she said, looking up at me, shamefaced; "But somehow it frightened me so. I ought to have gone and looked round the house, but I didn't dare. I tried to go on working, but from then on there was such an awful feeling—I can't describe it—as if there was something evil in the house—something close behind me—waiting to get its hands round my throat. Oh, Auntie, I know it sounds silly. It's the kind of thing I used to dream when I was a little girl—do you remember?"

Indeed I did remember. I took her on my lap and soothed her now just as I had done then, when she was a little sobbing girl awake and frightened in the depths of the night.

And then I told her she must go home.

"Auntie!" she protested; "But Auntie, can't I stay here with you for the night? That's why I came. I *must* stay!"

But I was adamant. I can't tell you why, but some instinct warned me that, come what may, she must not stay here tonight. Whatever her fear or danger might be

THE NEW HOUSE

elsewhere, they could never be as great as they would be here, in this house, tonight.

So I made her go home, to her lodgings in the town. I couldn't explain it to her, not even to myself. In vain she protested that the last bus had gone, that her old room here was ready for her. I was immovable. I rang up a taxi, and as it disappeared with her round the corner of the lane, casting a weird radiance behind it, I heaved a sigh of relief, as if a great task had been accomplished; as if I had just dragged her to shore out of a dark and stormy sea.

The next morning I found that my instinct had not been without foundation. There *had* been danger lurking round my house last night. For when I went to get my bicycle to go and help about the Mothers' Outing, I found it in its usual place in the shed, but the tyres and mudguard were all spattered with a kind of thick yellow clay. There is no clay like that between here and the village. Where could it have come from? Who had been riding my bicycle through unfamiliar mud in the rain and wind last night? Who had put it back silently in the shed, and gone as silently away?

As I stood there, bewildered and shaken, the telephone rang indoors. It was Linda, and she sounded tense, distraught.

"Auntie, will you do something for me? Will you come with me to the house tonight, and stay there while I do the painting and—and sort of keep watch for me? I expect you'll think it's silly but I *know* there was somebody there last night—and I'm frightened. Will you come, Auntie?"

There could be only one answer. I got through my day's work as fast as I could, and by six o'clock I was waiting for Linda on the steps of her office. As we hurried through the darkening streets, Linda was apologetic and anxious.

"I know it's awfully silly, Auntie, but John's still working late, and he doesn't even know if he'll finish in time to come and fetch me. I feel scared there without him. And the upstairs lights won't go on again—John hasn't had time to see the electricity people about it yet—and it's so dark and lonely. Do you think someone really *was* there last night, Auntie?"

I didn't tell her about the mud on my bicycle. There seemed no point in alarming her further. Besides, what was there to tell? There was no reason to suppose it had any connection....

"Watch out, Auntie, it's terribly muddy along this bit where the builders have been."

I stared down at the thick yellow clay already clinging heavily to my shoes; and straight in front of us, among a cluster of partially finished red brick houses, stood Linda's future home. It stared at us with its little empty windows out of the October dusk. A light breeze rose, but stirred nothing in that wilderness of mud, raw brickwork and scaffolding. Linda and I hesitated, looked at each other.

"Come on," I said, and a minute later we were in the empty house.

We arranged that she should settle down to her painting in the downstairs front room just as if she was alone, and I was to sit on the stairs, near the top, where I could command a view of both upstairs and down. If anyone should come in, by either front or back door, I should see them before they could reach Linda.

It was very quiet as I sat there in the darkness. The light streamed out of the downstairs room where Linda was working, and I could see her through the open door, with her back to me, just as she had been in my dream. How like poor Angela she was, with her pale hair and her white, fragile neck! She was working steadily now, absorbed, confident; reassured, I suppose, by my presence in the house. As I sat, I could feel the step of the stair behind me pressing a little into my spine— a strangely familiar pressure. My whole pose indeed seemed familiar—every muscle seemed to fall into place, as if by long practice, as I sat there, half leaning against the banisters, staring down into the glare of light.

And then, suddenly, I knew. I knew who it was who had cycled in black hatred through the rainy darkness and the yellow mud. I knew who had waited here, night after night, watching Linda as a cat watches a mouse. I knew what was the horror closing in even now on this poor, fragile child—on this sickly, puny brat who had kept *my* lovely, sturdy children from coming into the world; the sons and daughters *I* could have given Richard, tall and strong—the children he should have had—the children *I* could have borne him.

I was creeping downstairs now, on tiptoe, in my stockinged feet, with a light, almost prancing movement, yet silent as a shadow. I could see my hands, clutching in front of me like a lobster's claws, itching for the feel of her white neck. At the foot of the stairs now ... At the door of the room, and still she worked on, her back to me, oblivious. I tried to cry out, to warn her. "She's coming, Linda!" I tried to scream; "I can see her hands clawing behind you!" But no sound came from my drawn-back lips, no sound from my swift, light feet.

Then, just as in my dream, there were footsteps through the house, quick and loud; a man's footsteps, hurrying—running—rushing. Rushing to save Linda; to save us both.

LAST DAY OF SPRING

EVEN THOUGH HER eyes were still closed, Martha Briggs knew that the sun was shining. The warmth was creeping slowly, gloriously across the blankets, and any minute now it would reach her face. But she wouldn't open her eyes just yet. No, this was the loveliest bit of the whole day, lying here with Thomas, waiting for the sun to reach their faces. Strange how the sun seemed to shine every morning now that she was nearly ninety years old. Such lovely sun too—it must be spring, day after day. If only she could get Thomas into his chair by the window; but he was too heavy, her arms weren't strong enough to lift him any more.

Thomas.... What was it that was worrying at the back of her mind, spoiling this lovely lying still in the sunshine?

Then she remembered. Of course! It was Thursday. This was the day when that Welfare woman with the clumping shoes was going to come and take Thomas away.

Take Thomas away, indeed! Martha had never heard such nonsense! Hadn't he ever been ill before during their sixty years together, and hadn't she nursed him then? Of course she had—and before this clumping woman had been born or thought of, too!

She tried her hardest to remember what the creature had said. For a little while she could only remember the great shoes, and the snorting breathy sort of voice that was so difficult to hear. Then slowly the woman's words came back to her:

"It isn't that we're criticizing you, Mrs Briggs, not for one moment. We know you're doing your very, very best—you've done wonders for your age, I know you have. But you see—well, I'm sure you'll agree with me really—it isn't right, is it, that he should be lying like this at past midday, not been attended to, not even had his breakfast yet! And the room! ... You *do* see, don't you, Mrs Briggs? It simply is too much for you—it's *you* we're considering really, you know, just as much as him. And he'll be quite happy, I promise you, he'll have every attention...."

On and on went the voice in Martha's mind, and she almost smiled at the absurdity of it all. As if she and Thomas couldn't have their breakfast when it suited them! If they liked to lie like this in the sun for a little while first, whose business was it but their own?

Still, perhaps it would be a good idea, this morning, to teach that creature a lesson. She'd get up early and cook a good breakfast. Now, what would they have? An egg. Of course. She would fry an egg for Thomas. He would love that, with a bit of fried bread. She knew there was an egg somewhere, and he should have it. Then she would scrub the floor until the boards shone white in the sunlight; she would wash the curtains—she could almost see them now, billowing clean and lovely on the line. She would polish the chest of drawers, and rub the window till it shone. Too much for me, indeed! thought Martha: *I'll* show her!

But the sun was right on her face now in all its glory. It would be a shame to get up just at this minute, just while it was like this. She would lie and enjoy it for a minute or two longer....

Martha woke with a start. How tiresome! She must have dozed off, and now she would have to hurry to get everything done before that woman arrived.

She climbed stiffly out of bed and fumbled about for her dress. Where *could* it have got to? Then she remembered: of course, she had to sit quite still on the edge of the bed for a bit in the mornings, then things sort of straightened themselves out.

Her head was dropped a little forwards, and she could see lots and lots of floor. It was quite true; it was dirty. And what was worse, now that she was up all her enthusiasm for scrubbing it had drained away. The vision of sunlit, white-scrubbed boards was gone, and she could think only of the backbreaking weight of the pail, and the ever more perilous feat of getting down on to one's knees and then, somehow, getting back up again....

But at least she had found her dress. At least that woman would find her up and dressed this time, and Thomas with a good breakfast in front of him. She made her way into the kitchen and set about preparing the meal.

But how had the fat in the frying-pan managed to burn black and smoking in just that moment or two it had taken her to find the egg? How tiresome things were!

She poured the blackened mess away and started again, and this time it was wonderful. The egg was fried plump and golden, a little crisp round the edges, just the way Thomas liked it, and the fried bread was delicately brown. *That's* what he needed to build up his strength, a good breakfast like this every morning. It would be quite a job to buy an egg every day out of her tiny pension, but she'd managed it this time, and she'd manage it again.

Now to get it into the bedroom. Slowly—oh, so slowly, because the boards had grown so uneven and treacherous of late—she carried it across the landing and into the bedroom. First she must put it down while she got Thomas propped up comfortably on his pillows.

But when she tried to put the plate down on the chest of drawers she found to her annoyance that there was no room there. It was all cluttered up with stuff—what *was* all this rubbish? She looked more carefully—and a dull bewilderment gripped her. For on the chest of drawers already was a plate with a fried egg on it—ice cold and congealed. And another, and another and another—each with its loathsome wrinkled egg, staring at her like ancient eyes.

Something, half a memory, half a fear, made her turn, slowly, slowly, to look at the bed.

Yes, it was empty. Stark, staring empty. Thomas was gone.

She knew she must sit down on the edge of the bed and think this out. There was something—something she half remembered—something that made sense of all this.

It was the wrong Thursday! That woman had already

come on some other Thursday—last Thursday?—the Thursday before?—and had taken Thomas away.

Taken Thomas away! The import of the words burned into her. How *could* she have let it happen? She, who had defended her family against all comers: she who in her time had stood up to rent collectors, probation officers, school-attendance officers, bailiffs, all the lot of them—how *could* she have let this flatfooted woman take her Thomas away?

She must think, think. When did they take him? Where would they have taken him to? Where *did* that woman say?

The hospital. Of course, Thomas was ill; it must have been the hospital. She would go there right now and fetch him, fetch him home herself through the spring sunshine.

Such a long, long way to the hospital, and when she got there and sat down at last on the hard bench, how they did talk! One after another of them, flashing about in front of her, snapping out questions like firecrackers.

"No record of it." "No such admission"—the senseless words kept tossing about among them like paper balls—like little girls playing ball in a sunlit garden....

Sister spoke a little louder, still patiently:

"Do you understand? You must go to the enquiry desk, and they'll give you a form. You must fill in the patient's name and address, the date of admission...."

But Martha Briggs was no longer listening to her. Because right now at the far end of the shadowy stone corridor she could see Thomas. How well he looked! and —why—he was *running*, actually running towards her, with his dear grey hair all rumpled and his arms outstretched.

"Thomas!" she cried, in joy and anxiety, "Thomas, my darling, you mustn't run!—your heart! ..."

She drew one breath of sweet, cool air, and then somehow seemed not to need another; for now she too was running, lightly, lightly, like a young girl, like a bird, her feet skimming over the stone floor. How wonderful it was to run, and run, and run to meet your love.

"Will you *please* go to the enquiry desk—" Sister's voice broke off suddenly. A less expert eye than hers would scarcely have noticed the slight change as the old woman's head dropped a little farther towards her chest and the faint breathing stopped.

THE SPECIAL GIFT

Eileen glanced disconsolately at the little group cowering round the fire in her big, cold sitting-room. Only five of them tonight. It was the weather, of course, that was keeping most of the members away; not everyone was willing to battle through wind and sleet just for the pleasure of reading aloud to one another their amateur attempts at writing, and receiving some equally amateur criticism.

Still, thought Eileen, drawing her cardigan more tightly about her, it was a pity; these meetings weren't nearly so much fun with only a few. A crowd might have made it seem a bit warmer, too.

"Well—do you think we ought to begin, Mr Wilberforce?" she said, sitting down on the big horsehair ottoman next to the secretary, a plump, important-looking man in his fifties.

Mr Wilberforce glanced at the clock, rubbing his pink hands together.

"Only twenty past," he said. "Better give them a *few* more minutes. The snow, you know—buses—"

"*I* think we should start," piped up old Mrs Perkins,

peering out like a little aggrieved mouse from the depths of the fur coat she had refused to take off. "We've got a lot to get through this evening. I've brought one of my little tales of unrequited love, if you'd care to hear it. And I'm sure Miss Williams here"—she indicated a pleasant, vacantly-smiling girl on her right—"I'm sure Miss Williams has brought us another chapter of her psychological novel. And Mr Walters"—the pale young man lowered his eyelashes self consciously—"We hope Mr Walters is going to read us another of his Ballads of the Seasons. It'll be Summer this time, won't it, Mr Walters?"

"Yes, Summer," agreed Mr Walters, speaking rapidly and staring at the carpet. "But not Summer in the *conventional* sense, you understand. Now, *my* interpretation of Summer—"

A sharp, imperative ring at the front door brought Eileen to her feet, and she hurried eagerly out of the room. One more makes six, she was thinking, that's not too bad; all the same, I wish I hadn't cut all those cheese sandwiches....

A gust of wind and snow swirled into her face as she opened the front door, and the little dark man seemed almost to be blown in by it, so slight was he and thin in his flapping dark coat.

"You haven't been to these meetings before, have you?" Eileen was beginning and then stopped, for in the dimness of the hall the stranger seemed to be staring at her with a look of delighted recognition.

"We—we *haven't* met before, have we?" she went on awkwardly; and the little man seemed to rouse himself.

"Why—er—no!" he said hastily, shaking the snow from

his boots on the doormat. "No, indeed, I assure you! I just—had a feeling—"

Again he stared at her with that odd look of recognition in his eyes; and for some reason Eileen began to feel uncomfortable; for some reason she became very eager to escape from the piercing gaze of this stranger in the dimly lit hall.

"Come along and meet the others," she said hastily, and led him briskly into the sitting-room.

"Fitzroy is my name," the dark man introduced himself. "*Alan* Fitzroy." He glanced round the company with dark, sparkling eyes, and there was a little stir of interest. Not that anybody had heard of him, but something in the way he spoke made them feel that perhaps they *ought* to have heard of him. Perhaps, each of them was thinking, perhaps this at last is the *real* writer I have always hoped would turn up! The *real* writer who not only gets his own work published, but who will be able to tell me how to get *mine* published; who will recognize it as the masterpiece it is.... With such thoughts behind them, five pairs of eyes followed the little man as he moved towards the fire; eager hands drew up a comfortable armchair for him; eager voices plied him with questions.

But Alan Fitzroy was not very communicative. No, he didn't know any of the members of this group. No (modestly) he didn't write much—well, not *very* much. No, he hadn't brought anything to read—well, not really— anyway, let everyone else read something first, *please!*

And so the meeting began. Alan Fitzroy sat motionless his eyes closed. To everyone's disappointment he took no part in the comments and criticisms that followed each reading, and it was only when he was asked for *his* contribution that he roused himself.

"Well," he admitted, "I *have* brought a little thing. Actually, it's part of a larger work. I'm writing my autobiography, you see. In three volumes." He looked round the room expectantly, and there was an almost audible sigh of disappointment. This, somehow, didn't sound like a real writer; it sounded much more like an ordinary member of the group. However....

"I want you to understand," the stranger continued "That the whole object of this book is to bring the reader into real contact with my ego—to draw him—or her— into the life of my mind in a way which I believe has never been done before...."

As he spoke, he fixed his brilliant eyes on Eileen's face, and again she felt a little flicker of uneasiness—or was it even fear? Quite irrational, anyway, she assured herself; there couldn't possibly be a more harmless little man; and she settled herself to listen as he began to read from an enormously thick and dog-eared manuscript:

"The self-doubt and self-awareness of any repressed, frustrated childhood...."

The voice went on ... and on. At intervals Eileen glanced at the clock. She hoped that Mr Fitzroy wouldn't be offended if she went out and made the tea before he had finished. She hoped, too, that he hadn't noticed that Mrs Perkins was asleep inside her fur coat and might at any moment begin to snore. Mr Wilberforce, at Eileen's side, was fiercely making notes on the back of one of his own manuscripts. No doubt he was building up a pungent criticism of the weary verbiage through which this poor little man was ploughing.

"Go easy with him!" whispered Eileen softly—somehow it seemed very important to her that nothing should be said to upset the newcomer—"Remember he's new." But Mr Wilberforce only nodded his head irritably and went on writing.

Wasn't it *ever* coming to an end? But listen! At last! Those, surely, must be concluding sentences:

"In conclusion, to point the significance of these psychodynamic disturbances to my infantile ego, I must relate a nocturnal hallucination from which I used to suffer. Or, in common parlance, a dream. I dreamed I was walking along a passage, a long stone passage, my feet clanging as I went, as if I were wearing boots of steel—armour—something like that. At the end of the passage I knew I should find my cradle—the cradle I had as a baby—and I should have to get into it and lie down. And I knew that as I lay there I would see a face slowly rising over the side of the cradle, and the face would be mad. I never knew what would happen next, because I always woke up. In fact, I always woke up before I had even reached the end of the passage."

Abruptly the little man laid down his manuscript. He looked round triumphantly, and there was a little embarrassed silence, broken by a snore from Mrs Perkins.

"Well," said Eileen at last, wondering how to avoid hurting the little man's feelings, "it's a very *profound* piece of work, of course...."

"But it's too *long!*" exploded Mr Wilberforce. "And too self-centred—self pitying! You've used the word "I" eighty-seven times in the first four pages! I was counting!"

Alan Fitzroy turned on him indignantly.

"But I *have* to use the word 'I'! The whole book is about myself! I told you! The idea is to get the reader involved with *me*—to bring him right into my very mind, if you understand me—"

"I understand you perfectly," said Mr Wilberforce heavily, ignoring Eileen's nudges. "The idea is far from being a novel one. But, if you will allow me to say so, I think you are deceiving yourself. You speak of bringing the reader right into your mind, and in fact you don't even interest him. The whole thing is too wordy—too abstract. There's nothing in it to grip the attention."

The little man flushed angrily.

"Nothing to grip the attention?" he cried. "What about that dream, eh? Doesn't *that* grip your attention? Doesn't it?"

"Frankly, no," answered Mr Wilberforce. "It's simply an account of a childish nightmare such as all of us have had at one time or another. I appreciate that it may have frightened *you* as a child, but believe me, it won't frighten anyone else!"

The little man was trembling with rage now, and his face was scarlet.

"It *will* frighten people!" he almost screamed. "It *will*! I have a special gift for this sort of thing, I *know* I have! Let me tell you, a person once died of fright from hearing that dream!"

There was an awkward little silence. No one knew what to say to the absurd boast. Eileen got hastily to her feet.

"I think we all need a cup of tea!" she said, loudly and brightly, and escaped from the room. As she hurried down the passage to the kitchen, she became aware that Audrey Williams, the young psychological novelist, was following her.

"Thought I might help you, dear," explained Audrey; and added, as she piled cups and saucers on to a tray: "Whoever is that pompous little ass, do you suppose?"

"I can't think," said Eileen. "I felt rather sorry for him, really. He must have worked terribly hard on that stuff, you know. He had chapters and chapters of it written. I could see them."

"You're telling me!" giggled Audrey. "I thought at one point that he was proposing to read the whole lot! I nearly died...." Her voice trailed away, and both women were aware of Alan Fitzroy standing silently in the doorway.

"Funny you should say that," he said, looking straight at Audrey. "And you?" he went on, turning to Eileen. "Did *you* nearly die, too?"

Eileen flushed awkwardly. No wonder the poor little chap was bitter! It was a shame of Mr Wilberforce to have laid into a newcomer like that! She said, gently:

"Don't take too much notice of Mr Wilberforce. He's a very stern critic. He's like that to all of us sometimes, isn't he, Audrey?"

Audrey Williams nodded dumbly; and Alan Fitzroy spoke again, addressing himself to Eileen.

"And what did *you* think of my little effort? I sense a certain sympathy in you. Were you impressed by my dream?"

"Why—yes—" lied Eileen nervously, searching for words. "I thought it was quite—well—quite unusual. If you'd brought it in a bit *sooner*, though, instead of quite so much theory...."

"But I *do* bring it in sooner!" exclaimed the little man eagerly—he seemed to have quite recovered his temper—"I bring it in at intervals all through the book —just as it has come to me at intervals all through my life. But the reader doesn't know *why* I keep repeating it until the last episode! Don't you think that's a good idea? Keeping him in suspense, kind of thing?" He glanced with pathetic eagerness from one to the other of the two women; and Eileen, anxious to show the poor fellow a little encouragement, paused in piling biscuits on a plate to say: "Do tell us: What *is* the last episode?"

"Oh, well, you see, it was like this. This dream used to worry me, it really did. I'm not a nervous man— that is to say, my *type* of nerves, as I explain in the first eight chapters of Book Two—"

Hastily Eileen brought him back to the point.

"But the dream?" she said, counting out teaspoons on to the tray, and Alan Fitzroy continued:

"Yes, yes. The dream. What worried me, you see, was that each time I dreamt it I got a *little* further down the passage towards the cradle, where I knew I would have to lie down and see the Face. In the end, I was so worried about it, I told my wife. 'If only you could be with me, my dear' I said—just in fun, you understand—'Then I wouldn't be so scared'. Well, that very night I dreamt it again, and, believe it or not, she *was* there! She was walking along in front of me, wearing her old dark dressing-gown. She was a big woman, my wife—a big, strong woman, and she quite blocked my view of the cradle—the cradle where I knew the madness would begin.

So I felt quite safe. I didn't mind the dream a bit. And when I woke up"—the little man looked eagerly from Eileen to Audrey, like a conjurer bringing off a successful trick—"When I woke up, what do you think my wife told me?"

"Why, that she'd had the dream too, of course!" said Audrey promptly—wasn't that the obvious climax to the tale? But Alan Fitzroy shook his head. "No," he said. "No—that didn't come till later. No, she told me, that as she lay there, her head near to mine, she heard what she thought was my watch ticking under my pillow. But a funny, metallic tick, she said ... like a far off clanging of armour ... of steel boots. And then she knew that it came not from under the pillow but from inside my head. It was my boots clanging in my dream, you see, and she'd heard them."

Eileen and Audrey had drawn close together. Eileen's voice trembled a little.

"I think we ought to take the tea in—" she began; but the little man laid his hand on her arm beseechingly.

"Just a moment more!" he begged. "Just a few more words! After that, whenever I dreamed that dream, my wife would hear the clanging in my head, louder each night, until at last the night came when *she* had the dream, too! The clanging somehow forced her to go to sleep, she told me, though she tried hard to stay awake—and there she was, she said, right in my dream, walking down the passage in front of me, hearing my boots clanging behind her. What do you think of that?"

Eileen had recovered herself. Of course, this was just a piece of fiction on which he wanted her opinion. Mr

Wilberforce's crushing comments on the autobiography had stung him into trying to enliven it.

"Well," she said consideringly. "I suppose you could work that up into something quite dramatic. But however would you end it?"

"The way it *did* end, of course!" said the little man sharply. "It ended with my wife actually getting into the cradle. Naturally. It was *my* dream, wasn't it, and I *made* it end that way. Though there were one or two terrible struggles first. I told you, my wife was a big, strong woman."

"And—and what happens to her in it?" asked Eileen. "Does she see the face? And does she tell you afterwards what it was like?"

"Oh no!" said the little man, sounding surprised. "Of course not. She couldn't *tell* me any more after she'd got into the cradle. Naturally. She wasn't dead, but she was an imbecile by then. I found her in bed in the morning all curled up as she would have to be to fit into this little cradle, and she could no longer speak. Naturally. That *would* be the effect of looking at the face I am speaking of."

Eileen and Audrey looked at each other. Both noticed that the other had gone rather white; but the little man went cheerfully on, apparently quite unaware of their dismay:

"They took her away, of course, and put her into some sort of home. But it was all right, I knew I was safe now, because if *she* was in the cradle of course *I* couldn't be, could I? Each time I had the dream, there she was, filling up the whole cradle in her dark dressing-gown so that I couldn't even see it. I felt wonderfully safe for months.

"Until, one night, she wasn't there any more. That was terrible for me. I knew then she must be dead—and sure enough a day or two later I had word from the Home that this was the case. But come—" he seemed suddenly to rouse himself— "I mustn't keep you ladies from your tea —allow me!—" and taking one of the two trays he hurried off along the passage to the sitting-room.

Eileen and Audrey had only one thought—to get back to their companions. Hastily they loaded the other tray and a minute later they were in the sitting-room.

To their surprise, Alan Fitzroy was no longer there.

"Oh, he went as soon as he'd brought the tray in," explained Mr Wilberforce. "Said he had to catch a train to Guildford, or somewhere. Asked me to apologize to you— Why, what's the matter with you both?"

Eileen recounted briefly the story Alan Fitzroy had told them in the kitchen; and Mr Wilberforce looked grave.

"Fellow must be crazy!" he said. "I *thought* he looked a funny piece of work. Wouldn't have let him go if I'd known. Should have kept him, and rung the police."

"Oh, I'm only too thankful he *has* gone!" said Eileen. "I don't want a fuss. Besides, he *must* have meant it as fiction—though even so, he must be a *bit* abnormal to try—"

"Abnormal? Of *course* he was abnormal!" interrupted old Mrs Perkins. "I could see *that* in the very first moment! 'That's an Egalomaniac!' I said to myself—"

"Ego-maniac," corrected Audrey Williams, who was well up in the jargon needed for her novel. "Or do you mean megalomaniac—?"

The chatter went on, and the clink of tea-cups, and Eileen felt more and more thankful that the strange little man had gone. Suppose he had been the *last* to go instead of the first? She couldn't very well have turned him out....

Eleven o'clock now. One by one the members left, and at last Eileen was left alone.

"I must get all this cleared up," she thought, glancing wearily round the untidy room; and she began to move about collecting ashtrays and dirty cups. As she passed the ottoman she noticed Mr Wilberforce had left his gloves there; and so she was not surprised when a moment later the front door bell rang urgently.

But it was not Mr Wilberforce. The little dark figure had slipped past her into the hall before she had properly taken in what was happening.

She gave a little gasp of horror—and then recovered herself. After all, he looked a very innocuous little man standing there under the hall light and asking if he could look at a time-table. He had missed his last train, he said, but maybe ... on the other line ... a connection at Croydon, perhaps ... if he might just study the time-table a moment?

Eileen had no alternative but to lead him into the sitting-room and hand him the ABC. He settled himself in the armchair with it, and was soon thumbing through its pages with apparent concentration. Eileen went on with her tidying, trying to appear quite unperturbed. After all, she was saying to herself, what can he *do*? I'm twice his size, a big, strong woman....

Where had she heard that phrase before? The words

echoed in her head—"My wife.... A big, strong woman...."

It was then that she noticed how quiet everything was. The rustling of the pages of the ABC had ceased; and when she looked across at him, Eileen saw that Alan Fitzroy was asleep. His head was leaning back against the chair, his mouth was open, and his face was rather white.

"He looks queer!" she thought, stepping closer. "I think perhaps I *will* ring the police. Luckily the phone's in the kitchen, not in here; it won't wake him...."

And then she heard the noise. At first she thought it was a clicking in his throat, the prelude to a snore. But no; it wasn't a click; it was more a tiny clanking noise—distant—metallic—right inside his head.

Eileen did not stop to put down the tray she was carrying. The telephone! The telephone! That was the only idea in her mind as she hurried through the door and started down the passage to the kitchen.

But how loud the clanking sound had grown! It seemed to be following her out of the room—along the passage—clank—*Clank*—CLANK—

And where *was* the kitchen? How had this passage grown so long? And why were the walls of stone, and the floor too—stone that echoed to the clanking footsteps behind her?

She could not look behind. She could only hurry on, and on, and on, down the echoing passage, until in front of her she saw the end: the delicate muslin frills, stirred ever so slightly by an unseen breath. The lacy pillow, white and waiting. The coverlet, just recently turned back, in readiness, by an unseen hand.

With a strength she never knew she possessed, Eileen made herself stand still.

"It's a dream! It's a dream!" she told herself. "If I won't go with it, I'll wake up! I *won't* go with it! I *won't*! I *won't*! I *won't*!"

The clanking feet behind came nearer. Hands were pushing—pushing—fighting with her, and Eileen fought back—that dim, strengthless fighting of dreams, which yet somehow takes all a person's strength and more ... I won't! gasped Eileen silently, I won't. I won't I *won't*!

A crash that seemed to split her eardrums: she found she could open her eyes. She opened them on her own kitchen, on the tray of crockery lying smashed at her feet. Sweat was running down her face, and tears of pure relief came into her eyes.

A dream, of course! A sleep-walking dream brought on by that awful little man, and perhaps by over-tiredness. Why, it must have been part of the dream that he ever came back to ask for a time-table at all! Light-hearted in her relief, Eileen hurried back to the sitting-room.

No. That at least hadn't been a dream. But Alan Fitzroy was no longer sitting upright in his chair. He was sprawled on the floor as if he had been struck down by a violent blow, and blood was trickling from his head where it had struck the fender in his fall.

For one insane moment Eileen thought of that dream struggle at the edge of the cradle—*one* of them had had to fall—and then, collecting her wits, she rushed to telephone the doctor.

The doctor felt the little man's heart, his pulse; then

he shook his head.

"Not a hope, I'm afraid," he said. "You'll have to phone the police, my dear, and get them to find out where he comes from and everything. You go and phone them now, while I attend to the poor fellow," and he turned back to the prostrate figure.

But why was Eileen still standing there, motionless?

"Go on—*phone!*" said the doctor irritably. It was bad enough to be called out to a fatal heart attack at this time of night, without hysterical women delaying things. "Go *on*! The *telephone!*"

As if in a trance, Eileen moved towards the door ... along the passage to the kitchen. After all, perhaps it had been the doctor's watch chain making that tiny clanking noise. Yes, he must still be rattling his watch chain now—louder—Louder—LOUDER.

OLD DANIEL'S TREASURE

"OH, GRANPA, DON'T be *silly!*"

"For pity's sake, Pa, don't start *that* again! We can't stop in *every* evening, me and Lissa, just for your fads and fancies!"

The two female voices, one young and one middle-aged, spoke in unison; the two pairs of female eyes were fastened on old Daniel in a united glare of exasperation.

But Daniel's sharp old eyes could glare, too; and if there was fear behind his defiance, he wasn't going to let *those* two see it.

"I'm not asking you to stop in," he retorted with spirit. "It's not a pack of chattering women I want with me for a thing like this. It's a man I need—a man with a bit of strength in his arms. Where's that good-for-nothing husband of yours—?"—he turned on his daughter in sudden spite—"Why can't *he* stop in sometimes of an evening? Forgotten his own address, if you ask me!"

Edie flushed, as he had known she would; and the flush was unbecoming to her heavy face, deeply lined by the years of pretty frustrations and annoyances.

"You mind your own business!" she snapped. "Find

yourself a good book to read. Play a game of patience. And don't let me hear any more nonsense about footsteps when I get back! Footsteps, indeed! *Footsteps!*" In her rising annoyance she clipped the first syllable so that the word sputtered from her lips like the crackle of damp wood. "Come along, Lissa, darling," she added—in exaggeratedly gentler tones, for Daniel's benefit— "Time you got ready." The two of them fussed and thudded their way noisily from the room, and Daniel was left alone.

Well, not really alone, yet. For a few minutes longer they would be thumping and shuffling about upstairs, and then they really *would* be gone; he really *would* be alone in the ugly, over-furnished little house, full of shadows.

And it was Thursday evening. Three Thursdays running it had happened now; on just the evening when he was alone; on just the evening when the whole neighbourhood knew that he was alone, with Lissa off at the dance-hall—*dancing*, if you please, and her wearing a pair of trousers like a man—Lord, what a world it had become!—And Edie off to her Something-Or-Other Group —some piece of modern flapdoodlery which hadn't even a name to it, when he was young. Both of them out till midnight, and he, Daniel, alone. Alone, that is, except for the peculiar sound.

It began, usually, after they had been gone about two hours—maybe two and a half. Each time, when he first heard it, he tried to persuade himself that it was the wind; then that it was some big dog, snuffing and nosing round the back garden. Then, sometimes, as the clock ticked on, the ticks seem to ring with a strange, separate life in the little cluttered room, he would try to persuade himself that he was imagining it all; that there was, in fact, no sound. Then he would lean forward in his chair, straining his ears, his whole soul, in the hope of hearing nothingness.

And then, louder, unmistakeably, he would hear the sound again. Not, now, a sound that could be the wind; nor one that could be a dog, padding unconcerned on purposeless light paws. No, this was a purposeful sound; a measured sound; a furtive but unmistakeable shuffle of steps ... round to the back door ... to the side door; and then a terrible, breathing silence.

Ah, if only he were a young man again! If only he could leap from his chair, across the little hall, and fling open the door upon the intruder! Instead, there was the heavy labour of getting himself from his chair; of fumbling for his stick; and then the slow, intolerable progress across the room ... out into the kitchen.... No wonder that by the time he reached the side door there was no one to be seen. Only the dustbin, squat and monstrous, with its lid askew; and out of the darkness the strange, stale smell of a side entrance at night, with its huge, stifling walls, higher and narrower than any canyon.

The first time, it had not seemed to matter. A tramp, maybe. A drunk, lost and bemused in his search for home. But when it happened again ... and then again ... and always on a Thursday ... always when the old man was alone....

"Cheer—o, Pa!"

Edie, resplendent in her best clothes, and certain now of her evening out, could afford to soften a little. "Keep smiling! And don't go hearing any more footsteps! Remember what the doctor said."

What the doctor said, indeed! Daniel's secret throb of fear at the final slam of the front door was swamped in sudden rage. "Remember what the doctor said"—just as if the doctor had been able to get a word in edgeways, with Edie there in the surgery, self-appointed mistress of ceremonies!

"He suffers from a sort of clicking in his ears, Doctor," she had shouted—Edie always shouted when talking of other people's business—"He keeps thinking it's footsteps, he kind of gets nervy about it, if you understand what I mean, Doctor."

Well, if the doctor didn't understand what she meant, it wasn't for lack of being told. For twenty minutes they had sat there in the surgery, and she hadn't stopped talking once, not for a second. And she had only once lowered her voice—and then not very much—to say to the doctor, in piercing confidence: "We think perhaps he's going a bit—you know!—" and she had tapped her forehead meaningly, slyly, as if the slyness would, somehow, make the gesture incomprehensible to the patient.

Well, the doctor must have said something—or perhaps conveyed something by signs through this cataract of talk—for a bottle of eardrops and a little round box of pills had materialized, both of which old Daniel had thrown in the dustbin while Edie was out at work next day, and so that had been the end of that. "A little bit—you know—" indeed! If he wasn't careful Edie'd be going a little bit—you know—herself on of these days, with all this busy-bodying and nosey-parkering, and none of it doing her any good, either, she never found out anything she wanted to know....

Or did she? And if she didn't, ought he to tell her? Daniel's brow creased itself into deep furrows as he remembered that night—the Thursday before last—when she'd come home just before midnight and he'd told her about the footsteps.

"Oh, don't be silly, Pa," she'd said, briskly. "We've never had burglars here. What'd they come for? A precious lot *we've* got for anyone to steal!"

The resentful scorn with which she had glanced round the room as she spoke had seemed genuine enough; and Daniel had been half relieved, half dismayed to realize that she didn't after all, know about the emerald.

Daniel's brows creased more deeply still, pinching his face into an expression of strange intensity. Ought he, perhaps, to have told her of it, then and there? She would then, without doubt, have taken his story of the footsteps seriously, and would not have left him alone like this with so valuable a thing in his sole charge. He wondered, a little, why he had been so determined never to tell her about the emerald; why even now, when it was threatened, he could not bring himself to tell her.

Was it because she would have made him sell it? The thought of a jewel worth thousands of pounds lying idle, unused, in an old man's trunk would, he supposed, be too much for most women—too much, certainly, for a woman like Edie, who moaned so incessantly about the discomforts and privations of her narrow suburban life. But, on the other hand, what could she have done? She couldn't have *made* him sell it. She could have complained—scolded

OLD DANIEL'S TREASURE

—wept—anything she liked, but she couldn't have *made* him sell it, for it was his.

His? Well, of course it was his! Daniel's mind sheered away, almost in terror, from recalling the method by which he had acquired the emerald. Always, his mind did this. He would sit, sometimes, alone in his room, the old trunk open in front of him, and he would feel the lovely smoothness of the jewel, peering for minutes together into its unfathomable greenness, his heart almost bursting with the joy of possession. And then, in the middle of the ecstasy, an uncomfortable, half-frightened feeling would come over him: would lead him back, back through the uneasy labyrinth of thought, towards that time when the emerald had come into his hands; and if he did not switch his thoughts away quickly, all his joy in the great jewel would be spoilt, lost in the pangs of—

Well, of what? Not a guilty conscience, surely. What guilt could possibly attach to such a deed? It wasn't theft—it wasn't, really, a crime of any kind. Call it piracy, if you like—that was the very worst you could call it. Gay, swashbuckling, heroic piracy—a deed of many-coloured splendour against the drab background of London pavements. What man could be ashamed of such a deed as he looked back over the years? Why, he could remember as if it was yesterday....

No, he didn't want to think of the details. There was something about those details, even now, that he could not face. Something that made him uncomfortable—no, more than uncomfortable—frightened. There had been —he must admit it even if he could not understand it— there had been something terrible about the acquiring of that emerald, and now, if it was to be stolen from him, there would be something terrible about its loss. Oh, not the loss itself—that, of course, would be terrible enough in its matter-of-fact way; but there would be something more than that. Something that he did not dare to think of; something that he had known, in his heart of hearts, was lying in wait for him, inexorably, from the very moment when he had laid hands on its cool, fathomless loveliness....

Daniel awoke, conscious that he had dozed off for a while, and that the fire was burning low. Ten o'clock. Was it, then, the striking of the little clock that had roused him, with its noisy, insistent ping-ping, ping-ping?

He was now fully awake. It wasn't the clock at all; it was the telephone—ringing, ringing, ringing as if it would shake the house.

Stiff and feeble from sleep, Daniel reached clumsily for his stick, and, cursing his own slowness, made his way into the darkened hall, where the telephone was still ringing, wilder than ever it seemed in the surrounding darkness.

And, after all that, there was no answer.

"Hello!" Daniel kept repeating. "Hello. *Hello*. Speak up, cantcher?"

And still there was no answer. Only an eerie, purposeful silence; and then, faint and far away, a tiny, final *click*: and the instrument resumed its impersonal, senseless buzzing.

Angrily Daniel replaced the receiver. Dragging a fellow out of his comfortable chair like that for nothing! And at this time of night! No consideration, no manners—

that was the trouble with the present generation.

And all the time, underneath the bluster that he was trying to keep in the forefront of his mind, Daniel knew that his fear was growing. They would know, now, not that the house was empty, but that the old man was at home, and alone. The old man, who took a whole minute to get from his armchair to the telephone—*he* wouldn't be much hindrance! Perhaps they even *wanted* the old man to be at home.... Perhaps that was part of their plan....

Daniel wiped the sweat from his forehead, and looked in front of him, up the dimness of the stairs: beyond them, into the dimness of the kitchen: and behind him, towards the black gulf of the front door.

They would be coming tonight. He knew it; and as if this very knowledge had some deadly power of speeding his fate towards him, he heard, at that very moment, the sound.

Silently, swiftly—more swiftly than he had managed them for years—Daniel got himself up the stairs—into his bedroom—and closed the door. He did not dare to switch on the light, but his eyes, grown accustomed to the darkness, could see the big trunk well enough. In the darkness it seemed somehow menacing; like some huge, legless monster left over from some more ancient world than ours.

Daniel hesitated. He had formed no clear plan, as yet, for protecting his precious emerald; and, half to gain time, half from the sheer, blind instinct for self-preservation, he crept painfully into the wardrobe, and partly closed the door, leaving just a crack through which he might see and listen.

The darkness here was complete; the silence almost so. Here, among the fusty stir of the old garments, Daniel found it impossible to guess whether or not those light, stealthy footsteps were still prowling round the back door.

It was when they reached the stairs that he knew for certain; and with the certainty came a strange spark of triumph. "A clicking in his ears" indeed! "A bit— you know—" indeed! Edie'd sing a different tune when she found all the fish-knives gone, and the inlaid tea-caddy, and goodness knew what else beside! It was burglars right enough, and they could strip the house for all *he* cared: except, of course, the emerald....

The bravado left him, suddenly, with a horrible, disembodied lurch, like that of a sinking lift. For the footsteps were coming on ... round the bend of the stairs now. Creak ... Creak.... Regular and relentless as a clock ticking, slow as death.... And then the faintest shuffle ... shuffle ... on the landing. And it was then that old Daniel knew, knew without the help of conscious thought, that what was coming upon him was something more than robbery; more, even, than murder. No door, no lock could protect him now from the terror that was on its way.

Should he have flung himself out on them, then and there, as the torch wavered through the doorway, steadied itself, and then moved inexorably towards the trunk? Only the old can answer; for only the old understand what it is to be tied to a body they can no longer trust; to muscles that no longer spring promptly to action at the order of the will; to limbs that may falter, unpredictably, when the moment of action is at hand.

"They may not find it. If I just keep still, they may not find it...."

And now the two figures were kneeling over the trunk ... they were raising the great lid....

He knew the contents of the trunk by heart, and he could tell almost by ear what it was that they were taking. His scarcely-worn white shirts: the gold cuff-links: Aunt Mary's silver photograph frame: the little enamelled locket with his wife's picture inside: the great linen table-cloth that no one used any more. And, under that, they would find the emerald.

They had found it. For just one moment the torch flashed upon its translucent splendour, and then it dropped to the floor. Quietly, methodically, the two men packed the remainder of their booty, leaving the emerald where it lay.

And a minute later they were gone.

But the terror was not gone. In the empty house, now safe and silent again, old Daniel still crouched in the darkness of the wardrobe, not daring to move or think. For out there in the ransacked room the ghastly memory was waiting, ready to pounce at last—the memory that he had managed to fend off for all these months, in and out of the doctor's surgery, and under the whiplash of Edie's tongue. Now it could be fended off no longer, for there, not six feet away, lay the emerald, scorned and unwanted. Even burglars had no use for it. Just so must it have been scorned by whoever had thrown it into the gutter where Daniel had found it that rainy, dreamy evening all those months ago; found it, and snatched it up, joyful as a little child newly arrived in fairyland.

Edie had been right after all. He was a little bit—*you* know. This was the terror that had been waiting for him.

The ringing in his ears grew louder, and he prayed that it should be the harbinger of death: that death should come immediately, swift and kind, now that he knew that his mind had gone.

Heart failure, the doctor said; and no wonder. You could hardly expect the poor old gentleman's heart to survive the shock of finding burglars in his room. It was easy to understand how it had happened.

But what was *not* so easy—what no one, not even Edie or Lissa could understand—was why there should have been an old-fashioned green glass bottle-stopper lying on the floor a few inches from the old man's hand.

"And not even a bottle to go with it!" Edie remarked later; as if this added, somehow, to the tiresomeness of the whole affair.

FOR EVER FAIR

As soon as I saw him, I guessed that he wasn't a proper doctor. "J. Morton Eldritch, Authorized Practitioner"—that was how he described himself. But "Authorized" by whom? "Practitioner" of what? As I looked into the weak, slightly bloodshot blue eyes of the small man sitting opposite me, my suspicions grew.

Suspicions? Let me not deceive myself: they were more than suspicions. In my heart I had known all along that he couldn't be a real doctor. For one thing, real doctors don't advertise at all, let alone in the Personal column of a local paper; and for another, the claims made on behalf of this "Fantastic, unrepeatable offer" to "any woman who fears the loss of youthful attraction" had sounded just about as phoney as it is possible for a rejuvenation racket to sound.

Yes, he was a quack all right. But the thing that was disconcerting—the thing that was beginning to send nasty little shivers down my spine—was that he didn't even look like a *competent* quack. I may be a fool—desperation, in the end, turns any woman into a fool—

but I was not quite such a fool as to have supposed that J. Morton Eldritch's "Treatment", whatever it was, would work by any other means than by a sort of auto-hypnosis. By some sort of abracadabra, I supposed, he would make me *imagine* that I looked young and beautiful again; and that in itself might—might it not?—give me the sort of confidence a woman needs to win back the love of her middle-aged husband. Love that has been stolen from her by an innocent little smiling blonde, kitten-sweet and young as the morning.

But this shabby, shifty little man in front of me, with his pasty, ageless face and sleep-starved eyes, did not look as if he would be able to give anyone confidence in —anything. Where was the dark, hypnotic gaze that should by now be fixed on me, boring into my very soul? Where was the rich, mellifluous voice, warm with concern (however bogus) for my pitiable middle-aged problems? Where was the practised smile, the perfect teeth, the calculated aura of father-figure-cum-admirer that should by now be making me feel feminine and desirable again? Surely this was what one paid for in these rackets— with a bit of black-box, or relaxation, or what-have-you, thrown in?

Half-guiltily, as if afraid that he could read my thoughts, I averted my gaze from my unlikely-looking healer, and wished desperately that I had never come. Why had I been such a fool as to telephone for an appointment in the first place? And why, having once done so, did I not turn back hastily as soon as I saw the kind of street in which "Dr" J. Morton Eldritch had his "consulting rooms"? I had seen at once that it was a dead street.

There were no corner shops, no prams: just tall, blackened houses with secretive lace curtains, and in each doorway were displayed a row of lifeless bells, each bearing the faded traces of some vanished name, relic of grey anonymous weeks in some life or other that has long gone hence, and the street knows it no more. At No. 27 I had to ring four of these phantom bells before a fat, bedraggled crone in carpet-slippers dragged herself from some fastness in the bowels of the house to answer the door. She blinked at the unaccustomed daylight, stared with an apathy that went beyond rudeness as I explained my errand, and then, with a jerk of the thumb indicating that my destination was somewhere on one of the upper floors, she crept back into the dark hollows of the house, leaving me to find my own way upstairs.

And now, here I was. The tortuous, despairing courage which had brought me thus far was failing me, and I longed to escape. The room was sour and sunless; unwashed cups and milk bottles in which the last dregs of milk had long gone bad, stood about on ledges. The owner of the room himself looked sickly and defeated, unable to succour himself, let alone anyone else. But I could think of no excuse for leaving which did not sound insane. Already Mr—or "Dr" I suppose he would wish to be called—Eldritch was beginning to take down the particulars of my case in a dog-eared exercise book.

"Forty-one years old," he murmured aloud as he wrote. "Married—Husband in love with much younger woman —Tell me about her!" His rather high, nasal voice sharpened suddenly on the words, and he sat, pen poised, watching me from his bleary eyes.

"About her? About Edith?—Oh—Well. Let me see. She's very young, of course—about eighteen I'd guess—and *very* pretty, in a blonde, fluffy sort of way." As I began talking, I felt a certain optimism seeping back into my soul. After all, in a situation like mine there was nothing to be lost, and it *might* be that this odd, unprepossessing little man might have hit upon some trick, some dodge, that could help a woman—even if it was only a patent hormone cream neither more nor less useful than the rest. "It's her youth, I'm certain, that's the attraction," I continued, "because she's got nothing else. She's not intelligent, or amusing; she has nothing to talk about.... Whatever you say she just *smiles*, in a silly, empty sort of way...."

Edith's smile. I was describing it as well as I could, but there are no words, no phrases, which will quite convey the sickly idiocy of that smile. It may be just my jealousy, but I shall never forget the actual physical revulsion I felt when I first realized that Ronald—my husband—actually found that smile *attractive*. It was on a summer Sunday, and we were having tea on the lawn— strawberries and cream, if I remember rightly, and little sandwiches, and home-made raisin cake—anyway, quite a spread, because we had several neighbours in that day. I forget who brought Edith along—she was a niece? —family friend?—something like that—of one or other of our guests. Certainly *I* didn't invite her, I'd never met her before in my life. She came tripping across the lawn with a funny, light, half-running movement, bending forward slightly from her slender waist, for all the world as if she were about to fall forward into a pair of outstretched arms.

Ronald's. Not that Ronald's arms *were* outstretched, at that date; he was simply the man standing there, the man directly in line with the direction in which she moved. He caught her elbow, laughing, and helped her into a deckchair. And I mean *helped*. From where I sat, I could see how she was contriving to lean her fragile young weight full against him.... What had started as an automatic gesture of gallantry became, in that moment, something more. From then on, all that long, hot afternoon, Ronald stayed at her side, as if enchanted, dancing attendance on her in all sorts of ridiculous ways; arranging cushions at her back; draping and re-draping the absurd wisp of lacy stole that she affected—I suppose to protect those delicate white shoulders from the sun: *I* don't know —I thought all the girls *tried* to get sunburnt these days. Anyway, it proved to be a good gimmick for a man like Ronald; he was fascinated by all this delicate-plant pantomime, and utterly taken in by it. He told me afterwards how refreshing it was to meet a really *feminine* young woman at last; one who makes a man really *feel* like a man!

I don't know; he may not have meant it nastily; but anyway, I took it as a snide comment on *my* sturdy build and independent ways. I stormed at him for his unreasonableness in first expecting his wife to be able to redecorate the house, drive the car, and earn half the family income, and then turning round and sneering at her for not being a delicate, wilting little—

"I wasn't sneering!" he protested—truthfully or not, I do not know—but I took no notice. "A delicate, wilting little nincompoop," I concluded. "Like your precious Edith!"

"Leave Edith out of it!" he roared; and from then on I knew that I was lost. Oh, that particular row simmered down all right; and Ronald did not leave home; but from that moment onwards, he belonged to Edith. He knew it; I knew it; and, I suppose, she knew it. I say "I suppose", because even now I don't know if she realized how completely he was her slave all through that long, hot summer. She knew, of course, that he liked her company, because he was for ever calling on her, taking her for outings in the car, inviting her to our place for meals. Evening after evening, I remember, she would come tripping along up the garden path, leaning heavily on Ronald's arm; and smiling, eternally smiling, while he smiled down at her. God, what a pair of grinning fools they looked! What they found to talk to one another about I cannot imagine, because whenever *I* was there listening they would be exchanging remarks of such stupefying banality that I cannot conceive how Ronald—who is an intelligent man—could possibly endure it. "Not quite so damp today, is it, dear?" she would say, smiling up at him with her great goo-goo eyes; and he would beam, and squeeze her arm, as if she had said the wittiest thing in the world. And on the rare occasions when we *did* have any sort of reasonably intelligent conversation in her presence, she was far too cunning to expose her ignorance by taking part in it. Oh no. She just sat there, smiling and nodding like one of those nodding toys—and afterwards Ronald would tell me what a marvellous listener she is! Ugh! I hate the way she picks at her food, too, she won't ever eat a proper hearty meal at our table, but picks and pecks like a little bird, twittering about she can't eat this and doesn't eat that, until I, eating a normal helping, begin to feel like a great hog-like omnivore—and a bad cook into the bargain, because whenever Edith says in her little peevish-baby voice that she can't eat steak pie, or whatever, Ronald looks daggers at me for having cooked it, and pretends *he* doesn't like it either; so that I am grossly liking steak and kidney pie all by myself, while they smile their sickly, sensitive smiles at each other.

"And you feel," broke in Dr Eldritch gravely, "that by making yourself look just as young as this—Ah—this Edith—you will be able to recapture your husband's love?"

I stared. So absorbed had I become in the recounting of my troubles that I had almost forgotten where I was and for what purpose I was recounting them.

"Well, I—Well, it would help, obviously," I began. "But I wouldn't want—I mean, I have to think about it. Please tell me what the treatment consists of—"

"Oh, just a simple injection," said the little man, reaching absently on to a shelf in the alcove by his chair. "My syringe is already filled,"—and to my horror he unearthed from among the dusty piles of books and papers a naked, unsterilized syringe.

"Push up your sleeve," he ordered casually, "and come over here."

"No! No!" I cried. The man was not merely a fraud; he must be raving mad. "I can't—I don't want to! I mean," I added, desperately trying to humour him, "I need to think it over ... I'll let you know..."

"It may be too late then," he said, judicially, looking me up and down with his dull eyes. "You see, it only works on women who are still in fair shape, even though middle-aged. In your case—yes. I believe I could make you look, after one single injection, just as you did when you were eighteen. But once the body has *really* begun to deteriorate—" he shook his head. "No, it can't be done with a *really* ageing body. It has to be done by the time you are forty or thereabouts, or it's no good. And remember, Madam,"—he made a visible effort to instill some sort of enthusiasm into his flat, nasal voice—"Once you have been transformed by my method, you *stay* transformed. I mean, once the injection has taken effect, you will go on looking eighteen for the rest of your life, even if you live to be a hundred! Wouldn't you like that? Of course you would! Any woman would!"

I played for time. I was less frightened now. Madman though he was, he did not seem to be proposing to inject me against my will.

"I suppose you've tried it out?" I said chattily. "I'm not your first patient?"

He hesitated. "I'll be honest with you," he said. "This substance was invented by my grandfather, nearly a hundred years ago: and he tried it out, as you put it, with the most marvellous success on quite a number of people, including himself. If you want proof, let me show you a photograph of my grandfather, taken at the age of eighty-four...." He crossed the room and began rummaging among a huge pile of dusty volumes on an old horsehair sofa. "Look." He fished out an old photograph album and brought it over to me. "See? Not bad for eighty-four, eh?"

I looked at the picture of the eighteen-year-old boy in front of me, and wondered what to say. It could have been *any* eighteen-year-old boy of the nineteen-thirties. It proved nothing.

"He's very good-looking," I said feebly; and then: "If it worked so well, how was it that he didn't become famous, your grandfather? Why didn't this method spread all over the world?"

Dr Eldritch shook his head sadly. "The usual story. The world wasn't ready for such an invention. He was reviled—slandered—spent years in prison: and when he came out, he did not dare go on. He hid away his secret— and only by chance, and only recently, did *I* come upon it. I am hoping that now, perhaps, the world *is* ready for it; and that perhaps *you*, good lady, will have the courage...."

"No! No!" I stepped back a pace, and racked my brains for some way of keeping him talking while I watched my chance to dart out of the door.

"What happened to the others?" I gabbled. "The other people he rejuvenated?"

"I'm glad you asked that." The little madman was beginning to sound almost cheerful. "I can show you some 'Before and After' photos of his clients which will certainly convince you."

He flipped over the pages of the album until he came to a page where pictures of half a dozen middle-aged women, dressed in Edwardian styles, were juxtaposed to pictures of their younger selves—taken, evidently, at around the age of eighteen or so.

"You see?" he said triumphantly. "The older pictures were taken *first*, you see, and then...."

I did not question his topsy-turvy logic, or the validity of his argument. I did not dare to. Within seconds my mouth had gone too dry for me to be able to speak at all. For one of the pictures was known to me already— so well, so well. Out of the yellowing old print of seventy years ago, Edith's face smiled sweetly at me.

"Well, never mind," he concluded. "I'm not going to press you: I am only sorry, for your own sake, that you have decided not to avail yourself of my treatment. However, no doubt you know your own business best."

He bowed me out most politely; and he was right; I *do* know my own business best. All I have to do now is wait, and watch. When Edith smiles her baby-kitten smile, and clings to Ronald's arm, *I* can recognize, though he can't, the vacuous, empty smile of encroaching senility; *I* can see, in that cute, tripping little walk of hers, the gait of an old, old woman, keeping her balance as she goes; and when he helps her in and out of chairs, *he* thinks she is sweetly playing up to his masculinity; *I* know that she cannot get up without him, now that she is nearly a hundred years old. When she makes her little, artless remarks that he loves so much, *I* can see her second childhood coming.

He is taking her to a dance tonight; how sweetly she will lean on him, clutching him for support as her old limbs struggle to keep up with the music, and her lovely smile hides the confusion of dying thoughts that tumble through her fading mind. His arm will encircle a lovely, slender form so helpless with age that it can hardly stand. How soon will he realize that behind that lovely face the brain is going? How soon will the meandering, muddled fancies of old age break into the conversation in such a way that they no longer seem quaint and sweetly simple even to him? Soon, she will be dribbling over her meals as well as picking and pecking at them; soon, she will be incontinent, and will roam bewildered round the house at night, muttering of grievances that no one can understand.

But today she still smiles her sweet, vacuous smile, she still clings sweetly to his arm, and Ronald still loves her for it. He must wonder, sometimes, why I sit so relaxed and content now, watching them.

THE IRONY OF FATE

FOR A MINUTE Frances sat very still, the dry, stubbly grass of the embankment pricking through her thin dress, her fist still tightly clenched round the handbag that was no longer there.

A railway accident! I've been in a railway accident! She repeated to herself with a sort of bewildered pride. A real railway accident, and I wasn't frightened at all. It was—fun!... Wasn't it? She tried with all her might to remember exactly what had happened, but it was difficult. It had all been so quick—so noisy—and yet so quiet. That moment of absolute stillness before the carriage began to tilt ... before the white, contorted faces opposite her had begun to scream ... before the fat old gentleman who had spent the journey complaining wheezily about the service on this line had wrenched the door open and yelled to her "Jump! Jump for your life!" and had half dragged, half pulled her out with him.

Frances laughed a little to herself, dazedly, gratefully. Who would have thought that the old boy would have been so agile! I wonder what he thinks of the service on this line *now*! she thought shakily; I wonder if he is all right?....

It was only when she turned her head to look for him that Frances realized that she still had her eyes closed. With an effort she opened them and looked round.

Dusk was falling, and the first things she saw were her own feet, looming up out of the grass in their smart little red sandals. And her nylons! Wonder of wonders, her best nylons were unladdered—perfect! She giggled a little. Fancy being flung out of a train in a disastrous accident and not even ladder your nylons! I must be the cat with nine lives she thought—no, my *stockings* must be cats with nine lives—kittens with nine lives ... stockings. ... kittens ... kittens ... stockings ... stockittens ... She giggled again. That's rather good, she thought; I must tell someone....

To her annoyance, she found that her eyes were again closed, and again she opened them. This time she roused herself properly and looked about her, taking note of her surroundings. On either side of her stretched the steep bank of dusty grass; in front lay the wrecked carriage, its complicated and hitherto unimaginable underside exposed to view. It reminded her of a beetle fallen on its back ... at any moment one expected to see the upturned wheels kicking helplessly in the air....

But I must *do* something, thought Frances; I can't sit here all night. What *do* people do after an accident...? From the other side of the carriage, invisible to her, came a confused clamour ... hammering ... voices ... shouts. If you've been hurt, of course, they come and rescue you; but if you haven't ... if you're just sitting on the embankment, a bit dazed but without a scratch ... ?

Frances shook herself. Why, of course, if you can't do anything to help—and faced by the hugeness of the upturned carriage in the darkness Frances felt quite, quite sure that she couldn't do anything to help—you walk back to the nearest station and telephone your family, and ...

Your family. Michael and baby Susan. Michael, who had once loved her so tenderly, who would once have done anything in the world she cared to ask. Michael, who at this very moment must be waiting impatiently for her to get home and take over the care of Susan while he went to his wretched art class. Frances clutched angrily at the dry grasses. This art class of Michael's—*that* was what was coming between them and causing all the quarrels; not her "absurd possessiveness" as Michael called it. Was it "absurd possessiveness" for a wife to object to being left alone three evenings a week while her husband went and stared at who knows what beautiful models for hours on end? Hadn't she a right to feel neglected and ill-used? And it wasn't only the three evenings at the art class either, thought Frances resentfully; every moment of Michael's spare time at home was given up to the wretched business too. If he wasn't actually painting, with a grim concentration which excluded Frances and her conversation completely, then he would be messing about with his brushes at the sink, dripping oily splashes all over everything. Or he would be "doing up frames"—perhaps that was the worst horror of all, mused Frances. Scarcely a Saturday passed without him coming home in triumph with some huge cobwebby monstrosity under his arm which he had "picked up for a song—perfect when I've cut it down a bit for that seascape of mine."

"Cutting it down a bit" of course meant sawdust and plaster-of-paris all over the kitchen, and then having the thing lying about somewhere hopelessly in the way for the best part of a week while the glue dried.

When Michael had first got this craze for painting—nearly a year ago now—he had been eager to discuss it all with Frances and to show her all he did. But Frances, hoping to bring home to him his selfishness and neglect of her, had refused to take any interest; and of late he had spoken of it very little to her. Instead he had taken to bringing that frightful woman with the earrings back with him after the classes and arguing with her till all hours about post-impressionism, or about so-and-so's pre-Raphaelite tendencies. Frances usually went to bed on these occasions, to show her boredom and disapproval; but more often than not he didn't even notice, so engrossed was he in talking to this creature....

The crash of splintering wood and a shout recalled Frances to her situation. It was quite dark now. She ought to be making her way home. If only I'd been hurt! she thought suddenly. If only I was being carried to hospital, dangerously injured, *then* Michael would be sorry! *Then* he'd wish he hadn't neglected me all these months! She gazed almost longingly at the black hulk of the wrecked train; and in that moment, as if it had crawled out from under the carriage as a worm crawls from under an upturned stone, an idea crept guiltily into her mind.

That would show him! All I have to do is—nothing!

If I don't telephone ... don't go home ... just disappear for the evening, *then* perhaps he'll be sorry for the way he's treated me!

For, of course, Michael was sure to hear of the accident. He was sure, too, to realize that she must have been on that train—when she went to her sister's for the afternoon she always came back on the 6.25. She pictured Michael frantically telephoning one hospital after another ... dashing to the station ... to the scene of the accident.... The picture brought tears to her eyes, and yet filled her with a warmth and peace she had not known for months. The thought of it was like food and drink to her, like fire and shelter on a stormy night. For one evening at least Michael's attention would be riveted on her, and on her only. His anxiety, his fear, they would be nothing more than a measure of his love. She would know at last— and he would know—that she was needed—missed; that he loved her—could not do without her.

Frances stirred uneasily. An opportunity like this would not occur twice in a lifetime. And it would be so easy, so temptingly, irresistibly easy. Just walk away into the darkness. And in the morning she would return home and bask in Michael's joy at her safety, his remorse, his tenderness, his renewed willingness to do everything she wanted for evermore.

But what about the questions she would have to answer? Why, if she wasn't hurt, hadn't she come straight home? Frances hesitated, but only for a moment. Why, she could say she had been stunned—lost her memory—anything. All sorts of things could happen to people involved in a Railway Accident. Already the phrase had taken on the quality of a charm—a talisman. "I've been in a Railway Accident"—it was like a badge one could wear as some women wear their beauty—a badge exempting them from all ordinary rules and standards.

Concussion! The world flashed into her mind like an inspiration. You behaved in all sorts of queer ways when you had concussion, and there need not be any mark to prove you had it. Some friend of her sister's—hadn't she had concussion once from falling off her bicycle, and not even a bruise to show for it? And that man—the one who was hit on the head by a falling ladder, and then walked several hundred yards without knowing anything about it before he collapsed?

Yes, that was the thing. She would let them think she had had concussion, and had just managed to stagger a little of the way home before she collapsed in some unfrequented spot where no one had happened to find her. And when she returned with her story in the morning Michael would be so tender ... so solicitous. She would be surrounded by his protective love once more as she had been when they first married. He would realize how he had neglected her ... he would give up all this painting nonsense, and that black-haired woman with her jangling jewellery would never come to the house again....

The bank was steep, the dry autumn grass slippery, and more than once Frances was afraid that she would be seen before she reached the top. But she need not have worried. Everyone was far too busy to look up and notice the small figure creeping away into the darkness....

Houses. Rows of houses. The accident must have taken

place just outside the station, then. Her own station? The one just before hers? Frances slowed her hurrying steps and tried to think. What was the last station they had passed before...? She couldn't remember—had probably not even noticed, for throughout the journey, throughout the afternoon her mind had been filled with angry, resentful thoughts which shut out everything else. Michael's voice at lunch-time, casual, indifferent, his thoughts already on the half-finished canvas in the corner:

"All right, you go to Emily's if you want to. I'll keep an eye on Sue and give her some tea. But for goodness sake be back in time for me to get to my class at eight!" Nothing about missing her—nothing about wishing that she would stay at home with him on his one free afternoon in the week. And urging her to come back early not because he wanted *her*, but simply because he wanted to go to his class!

The thought stiffened Frances' resolution, and she walked on more firmly along the hard, tiring pavement. A warm triumph flowed through her. This evening he would *not* be going to his class; this evening he would *not* be bringing that woman back for one of their interminable talks. She pictured him waiting, the hated easel folded under his arm, his eyes on the clock, first irritable ... then uneasy ... then....

But how cold it was! It must be getting late. A little wind had sprung up, damp with autumn, and played spitefully round her bare head, making her ears ache, her eyes sting, her whole head throb. She was tired too, terribly tired. She must have walked a long way along these dreary streets of poorly lighted houses, all exactly the same. This surely couldn't be her home town, or she would have come across something she recognized long ago. Where could it be? Which of the towns on the branch line from Emily's would have these miles and miles of mean streets on the outskirts, all the same, and so poorly lit?

For the first time Frances began to feel doubts about her decision. Not about its rightness—that was a question she had chosen not to face just yet—but about its practicability. Easy enough to decide to stay out all night and give your husband a fright—but *where* do you stay, what do you do? Sit on a bench? But she hadn't bargained for this treacherous damp cold eating into her very bones. Keep walking about? But already Frances was tired— achingly tired.

A doorstep, temptingly sheltered from the wind, loomed in front of her, and without further thought Frances sat down to rest her aching limbs. If only she could find her way to the main shopping centre of this dreary place she might find a café where she could sit and at least be warm. Then she remembered that her handbag was lying somewhere buried under the wreckage of the train. She had no money—not even the price of a cup of coffee. She shivered, and drew her inadequate summer jacket more closely round her. How silly of me, she thought, to go off to Emily's in summer things on a September afternoon. But then it was so lovely and sunny when I started, and I couldn't have known that— well, that I was going to stay out all night.... A tent and a sleeping-bag would have been the things to bring if only I'd known....

Frances started awake, stiff and shivering. How long had she been asleep? She had a momentary wild hope that it might be morning, that the long vigil was over and it was time to rush home to Michael's warm, repentant arms, to bask in his sympathy.

But no. No flicker of dawn had crept into the black, starless sky, and Frances felt alone as she had never felt alone before. And as she sat, waiting for the mists of sleep to clear, she became conscious of a great fear. At first she could not place it. No stealthy footsteps approached along the silent street: no rustling in the dusty privet bushes at her side could account for her straining ears, her suddenly beating heart.

Like a searchlight, the fear quivered up and down the silent street and then settled, it seemed to Frances, right beside her ... on top of her ... blazing into her very soul.

She knew now what she was afraid of. She was afraid of this woman, sitting here on the doorstep. This woman who, to bolster up a childish pride, could condemn her husband to a night of tormented anxiety; could make capital out of a public disaster; and who, well and strong, could scheme to go home and extract sympathy for invented injuries....

What kind of punishment would the Fates have in store for such a woman? The irony of fate. Where would that irony lead them to strike, and strike with all their age-old pagan power?

Susan? Michael? Frances did not doubt that the Fates

knew her vulnerable spots; but which? or both? Oh God, what will happen to them? she moaned; perhaps what *has* happened? Out of the dark street the little cruel wind whipped past her face again, like the first messenger of a cold and ancient power, inexorable.

What *could* have happened? Her mind raced wildly over the possibilities, and then pounced. Of course! *That* was the punishment that the Fates would have chosen for her; a punishment so neat, so fitting to the crime.... They would have arranged that Michael, distracted with worry, should dash out to some hospital—to the scene of the accident—somewhere—leaving Susan alone. And Susan, left alone—well, what are the things that can happen to an eighteen-month old baby left alone in the house? She would have fallen downstairs? Or into the fire? Pulled something heavy down on top of herself? There were no end to the possibilities. Frances knew only one thing for certain. She must go home—now—at once—and tell Michael everything—if it was not already too late! If only she knew what time it was; but she might have been asleep on the step for hours or only for five minutes. The black sky gave no clue, and neither did the deserted street.

"Michael, Michael!" she moaned aloud; and the name somehow seemed to give her strength. Almost as if she was being lifted by some power outside herself, Frances found herself on her feet and hurrying through the darkness. All the stiffness seemed to have left her limbs and she was running—not at random, as she had feared in this maze of unfamiliar streets, but with a curious feeling of certainty that this was the right way home.

And she was not deceived. Sooner than she would have believed possible, she found herself turning a corner into the familiar shopping street where only that morning she had been wheeling Susan in her push-chair. Susan, well and happy in the sunshine. Sunshine. Susan, as yet untouched by the finger of Fate moving relentlessly through the night....

A rush of icy wind met Frances as she turned the corner into her own road, and it seemed to her like the breath of Fate itself; the breath that had blown cold, cold through the centuries, freezing and splintering the lives of arrogant mortals, until tonight it had reached this road, this house....

Even before she could see them, Frances knew that the windows of her home would be black and silent; that no light would be shining through the fanlight of the door. Somehow she seemed to have known too of the stillness that would fill the little hall as she stood there in the darkness. A stillness like the stillness of the carriage just before it began to tilt. She could almost imagine that the floor of the hall was tilting now ... rising ... slanting—tipping everything she loved down some black interminable staircase into a bottomless nightmare.

But there was not only silence in the house—the silence of a cavern where no living creature has been able to survive. There was also a faint, disturbing smell in the air. For one wild moment of hope Frances thought it was the smell of wet paint—the smell that she had always complained about, but which now would have brought her comfort past describing. A smell that meant life—that meant Michael—that meant the boyish enthusiasm, the gay vitality that had been the very light and backbone of their home, and she, Frances, had never known it! She had basked in it, lived on it, and yet never noticed it, so busy was she resenting the trifling inconveniences that went with it, grudging the tiny efforts it demanded of her as some miser might grudge the trouble of drawing aside a curtain to let in the blazing sun of June.

Wildly, Frances reached her hand along the wall to find the light switch, but it encountered nothing; and somehow she dared not take another step in the darkness —a step that might send her headlong down that phantom staircase winding down, down, down into unimaginable blackness.

The smell had grown stronger. It seemed to be seeping out of the darkness all round her, sweetish, sickening, tasting of doom. Surely Michael couldn't have...? In his despair at thinking her dead could he...? Would he...? And with Susan here with him...? The strange smell grew thicker—it seemed to press upon her in the darkness like a suffocating blanket. She gasped for breath, and far away a sort of thudding sounded in her ears ... louder ... louder ... thud ... *thud* ... THUD ...

"She's coming out of the anaesthetic nicely now," called a brisk voice. "You can come in and see her now if you like."

Frances struggled to open her eyes The thudding sound was still going on, but she recognized it now as her own heart. The sweetish smell of the anaesthetic had almost cleared, and a moment later she felt Michael's hand in hers and his face against her cheek.

"Michael!" she gasped hoarsely, "Are you all right?

Are you alive—and Susan?"

"Darling, of *course* we're alive! It's *you* who were in the accident, not us! Oh, darling, I've been so terrified—"

"Michael, I know, I'll never forgive myself! I was pretending to have concussion to make you...."

"Darling, hush! You weren't pretending, you *did* have concussion, and pretty badly too. You seem to have managed to stagger as far as the Station Cottages just by the line there—they found you unconscious on a doorstep there an hour or so afterwards."

"An *hour*? The Station Cottages? But I was walking for hours, through streets and streets of little houses, all the same."

Michael spoke slowly.

"It must have seemed like streets and streets because you were so ill," he said gently. "But actually it was only those five cottages—they *are* all the same. They told me that when they lifted you up you called out for me—you must have staggered along there trying to find me—Oh, dearest...!"

Frances tried to speak. She remembered that moment of calling out Michael's name, and the feeling of being lifted up by some outside power. But trying to find him! When the only plan in her mind had been to escape—to hide—to give him a good fright!

And yet—and yet? *Hadn't* she been trying to find him? Trying to find the love and closeness that had been missing between them? True, the way she had chosen to look for it was a twisted, dishonest way; childish, and childishly cruel. She would never look that way again. But

THE IRONY OF FATE

there were other ways ... honest, adult ways ... shining, sunlit ways, strewn with bright canvases, with sawdust and splashes of paint ... with laughter and gay discussion far into the night....

"And all the time I *did* have concussion!" murmured Frances. "Talk about the irony of fate!" She was nearly asleep now, and as in a dream she heard Michael's voice:

"... I was getting quite frantic, and there was this confounded old buffer still in the telephone booth bellowing down the receiver. He came out muttering curses about the telephone service in this area...."

"I'm so glad *he* was all right too," murmured Frances; and it didn't matter that Michael couldn't understand a word she said. Already an understanding more important than words was spreading like sunlight across the bed between them.

THE BABY-SITTER

DAPHNE COULD NOT have told you what the play was about. Her only thought as the curtain fell after the first act was: Fifty minutes are over already; in another two hours—perhaps less—I shall be able to go home and find out what has happened. Find out if this strange premonition of disaster—this sense of dread which grows stronger with every passing minute—is just the foolish fancy of an over-anxious mother, or if...

She stole a cautious glance at Tim as the lights went up. It had been Tim's idea, this evening out together—the first one they had had for months.

"This is absurd, Daphne," he'd said, "I know it's more difficult leaving Sally now we haven't got your mother just round the corner, but hang it all, the kid's nearly four. Surely by now she can be left with people she doesn't know so terribly well?"

And Daphne had agreed—in theory. But in practice it all seemed fearfully difficult. Most of Daphne's friends were tied up at home with children of their own, and those who weren't—well, thought Daphne, one can hardly

THE BABY-SITTER

ask busy, childless people to spend an evening baby-sitting when there is nothing you can offer to do for them in return.

Tim, of course, thought that was silly.

"Just ask them," he kept saying. "They can but say No." Impossible to explain to a man the diffidence one felt about laying oneself open to such refusals; the humiliation one would feel if Sally chose just that night to "play up" and keep the baby-sitter running up and down stairs with glasses of water, extra blankets, and reassurances about goblins, wolves, and "The Hen with Great Big Eyes."

The Hen with Great Big Eyes was Sally's pet terror. What had first put the idea into her mind Daphne could never find out—whether it was a dream, a picture, some story Sally had heard at her nursery school—or whether it was simply Sally's own rather over-active imagination. Whatever it was, the nights for several months past had been broken periodically by wild screams from Sally's room.

"The Hen, Mummy! The Hen with Great Big Eyes!" and Daphne would rush upstairs to find Sally sitting up in bed, flushed and shaking—sometimes the terror would even make her sick—and only after many minutes in Daphne's reassuring arms would the trembling cease and Sally settle peacefully to sleep again.

"Enjoying yourself, darling?"

Tim's hand laid caressingly on her own filled Daphne with compunction. What a fool I am! she thought angrily; spoiling the evening by worrying like this when he's taken all this trouble, and got these marvellous seats, and even found a baby-sitter for us himself.

"Of course, darling, I'm loving it," she said; but even while she was speaking her mind still followed relentlessly its single uneasy track.

"He's even found a baby-sitter." The chill, uncertain dread trickled again down her spine as the lights dimmed and the curtain rose once more upon a blur of moving figures; and voices as meaningless to Daphne as if they were speaking Hindustani beat once more upon her ears.

I'm being ridiculous, she told herself for the hundredth time that night. I've got absolutely nothing against the woman. Tim's boss says she's marvellous—surely he'd know if there was really anything queer about her? Surely he wouldn't have recommended her to Tim as a baby-sitter if he hadn't been absolutely sure...?

Daphne racked her brains to remember everything Tim had told her about this Mrs Hahn.

"She's a refugee from Poland, or Hungary, or somewhere," he'd said cheerfully. "And she works for the Children's Something-or-Other. So it stands to reason she must be good with children."

Daphne had pointed out drily that plenty of people work in the offices of Children's Something-or-Others without ever setting eyes on a child, but Tim had brushed this aside:

"Well, anyway, Barker says she's marvellous, he's known her for years. A most reliable woman, he says, very efficient, and wonderful in any kind of emergency. I've rung her up, and she says she can come as early as we like on Saturday—she'll even put the kid to bed for you! Just think, Daphne—we can get away early and have a slap up dinner before the show! We'll make this a real celebration!"

Touched and excited by all these plans for her pleasure, Daphne had allowed Tim's enthusiasm to override her uneasiness at the idea of leaving Sally with someone, however well-recommended, whom she herself had never met. And in the excitement of altering the evening dress she had not worn for three years; of having her hair shampooed and set at the hairdressers for almost the first time since Sally was born, the uneasiness faded. It did not return until the very evening they were to go. Not, in fact, until she heard the strange footsteps clicking up the front steps and heard the short, sharp ring piercing peremptorily through the house.

The first thing that shocked her when she opened the door was that Mrs Hahn should be so tall. Nearly six feet she must have been, and wearing high-heeled shoes as well. So at first, peering up at her in the fading evening light, Daphne could get very little idea of her face. The gruff, foreign voice seemed to Daphne far from reassuring; so also did Mrs Hahn's movements, so swift and large, her arms flailing like great wings as she took her coat off in the hall.

"She looks like a windmill!" thought Daphne ungraciously as she hung up the heavy coat and led the visitor into the living-room. There, under the bright light, she got a second shock. For though Mrs Hahn was barely forty, her hair, eyebrows and eyelashes were quite white; and her huge dark eyes seemed to glitter with extraordinary brilliance against such a background. And what an odd way she does her hair, too, thought Daphne—quite short and straight, and brushed back and up from both sides to form a sort of ridge on top, making her look even taller than she was already. What with that, and her long sharp nose and sallow skin—she really is terribly plain, thought Daphne pityingly, and yet with a disconcerting qualm of fear.

It had been arranged that Mrs Hahn was to come early, so that Sally could get to know her before being left in her charge. The moment the little girl came into the room, Daphne knew exactly what was going to happen.

"I don't like that lady!" said Sally, loudly and clearly, and backed against her mother's skirt.

"Come along, darling, she's a very nice lady, she's going to have a nice little game with you...."

Daphne wondered as she spoke if her words sounded as hollow to Sally as they did to herself. But before Sally had time to make any more protests, Mrs Hahn's voice broke in:

"I wish to draw a picture," she announced, and taking a pencil and paper from her bag, she set to work with an air of complete absorption, apparently unaware of Sally's presence. After a moment Sally's curiosity overcame her fears, and she began to sidle across the room towards Mrs Hahn. Daphne seized the opportunity to dash upstairs to Tim. She found him plunged half inside the wardrobe, looking for his tie.

"Tim!" she gasped in an urgent undertone; "Tim, I don't like her!"

"Don't like who?" Tim's voice came muffled from among the hanging garments.

"Her. This woman. Mrs Hahn. I don't like her."

THE BABY-SITTER

"You're as bad as Sally!" said Tim cheerfully, emerging from the wardrobe. "Why don't you like her? What's wrong with her?"

"Well—I—" Daphne was taken aback. If you couldn't see at a glance what was wrong with her, how could one explain?

"Well—she's so tall...." she began weakly, and was silenced by Tim's roar of laughter:

"Well—that's good, I must say! I never heard there was a maximum height for baby-sitters! You're mixing them up with jockeys, darling!"

Daphne wriggled away from his caress.

"It's all very well to laugh! You *must* know what I mean! She's so—so sort of queer.... Her hair's all white, and done that queer way!"

But Tim was laughing again, louder than ever.

"Well, honestly, darling, if women are to be judged by whether they do their hair a queer way there won't be many of them left to approve of! Look at your friend Brenda! First she had it all bits and pieces as if a two-year-old had been at it with the dinner-knife, and now she's got it all scraped up in that queer lump...!"

Daphne gave it up. How could you explain to a man the difference between Brenda's gay enthusiasm for odd fashions and the unbecoming queerness of this woman's hair—the unfeminine indifference with which it must be brushed back every morning, those long, flapping arms brandishing the brush....

"Tim—I'm sorry. I'm frightened of leaving Sally alone with her. Sally says she doesn't like her, and they say children can always tell...."

Tim interrupted again, this time with a note of irritation in his voice.

"Look, Daphne, you know as well as I do that Sally always makes a fuss about strangers. That was the whole idea of getting the woman to come early. They're probably getting on like a house on fire by now. Let's go down and see."

Though "getting on like a house on fire" was an exaggeration, Sally did seem to have got over her first dislike of Mrs Hahn. She was standing, solemn and a little guarded, beside the small table at which Mrs Hahn sat drawing a cat with swift, strong strokes. As they watched, Mrs Hahn paused to sharpen her pencil. It seemed to Daphne that the blade of her out-size pocket knife flashed with uncanny speed, and in seconds the pencil was needle-sharp.

The clapping and laughter broke in on Daphne's thoughts, but only for a moment. The sounds of the theatre faded again, and all she could hear was the slam of the front door—that awful final slam as they set off, leaving Sally alone with Mrs Hahn. Even then, thought Daphne, even then I could have turned back. Shall I regret all my life long that I didn't have the courage then and there to ignore Tim's anger and disappointment, to ignore Mrs Hahn's shocked resentment, and to run back up the road into the house and say: No, I'm not going. I'm staying with my child tonight.

Daphne stirred in her seat. No, she thought, no, I couldn't have done that, because at that point I hadn't begun to be really frightened. Uneasy, yes, but not frightened as I am now. Not filled with this growing dread, this mounting certainty that something is wrong—something has happened to my child.

Do I believe in presentiments? Daphne pondered the question. Do I believe that once or twice in a lifetime between human beings bound as closely together as mother and child, there can be a mysterious communication, beyond the understanding of science? Do I believe that in extremity of fear or danger a desperate voiceless message can be carried from mind to mind—a last frantic appeal for help?

Daphne's mouth was dry. I must pull myself together, she told herself; I must be reasonable. How could anything possibly be wrong? Mr Barker knows the woman; he's recommended her. She looks a bit odd, it's true, but after all Tim has explained that....

Suddenly her heart seemed to stop beating. Suddenly Tim's cheerful words came back to her with a new, a terrible implication. What was it exactly that he'd said as they stood together in the foyer before going up to their seats?

"You know, Daphne, I didn't tell you before, but since you're worrying so much about her white hair and so forth, I'd better tell you, she's had a pretty bad time in her life. During some revolution or other she was involved in helping to get a party of children across the frontier under the noses of the sentries. Most of them got through all right, but one of them—her own little girl—was killed. I don't know the details, but I believe they were pretty harrowing. About Sally's age, the child was. So you can't wonder that she looks older than her age. Who wouldn't, after an experience like that?"

At the time the explanation had seemed reassuring; but now, sitting in the darkened theatre, weighed down by an intangible foreboding, a new and horrible thought came into Daphne's mind. If a woman's own child had been killed—perhaps brutally murdered; perhaps under her very eyes—what is that woman going to feel at the sight of another child of the same age, happy and healthy in a warm safe home? What black feelings of hatred and jealousy are going to stir in that woman's heart—what rage and bitterness? What actions might she not be capable of, perhaps even against her conscious will ... driven by dark subterranean impulses beyond her control? Daphne saw again the gleam of the great pocket knife as it sharpened the pencil with such swift, such deadly skill.

And Sally. Sally asleep in bed, rosy and trusting. Or perhaps was waking—frightened—calling for comfort after a dream about the Hen with Great Big Eyes.

Another thought came to Daphne, a thought so sickening in its horror that she began to tremble from head to foot.

"Tim!" she whispered frantically, "Tim, what's Hahn the German for?"

Tim frowned.

"Ssh-ssh!" he hissed back.

But driven by terror Daphne persisted, oblivious of disapproving glances from neighbouring seats.

"Is Hahn the German for hen?" she whispered, hoarse with fear.

"Ssh! I expect so. Shut up!" whispered Tim peremptorily, and turned back to the stage.

THE BABY-SITTER

The Hen. The Hen with Great Big Eyes. Those long arms, flapping like wings ... the long sharp nose like a beak ... even the hair brushed up in a ridge like a chicken's comb ... and the huge dark eyes, shining. Was it this that had haunted Sally's dreams all these months—some strange foreknowledge such as perhaps can come in the very young, their minds receptive and open to impressions of which we know nothing? A knowledge that one day it would happen: one day—no—one night— there would come creeping up the stairs a beaked, inhuman creature, its grey comb quivering, its great arms raised like wings, and in one of them a knife, shining. And what strange cackling noise might it not make in its gruff throat as it crept towards the bed....

Daphne was on her feet. The curtain had fallen after the second act, and she dragged Tim from his seat.

"Tim!" she almost screamed, "Tim, we must go home now, this moment. Something's happened to Sally! I know it! I can feel it in my bones!"

Ever afterwards she remembered the drive in the taxi through the lighted streets, Tim sulky and protesting beside her; drawing up outside the house, dark and silent, and Tim's caustic comment: "You see? No flames coming from the windows; no blood running under the door!"

But when they got inside the front door, something in the darkness and the silence arrested even Tim's attention. Suddenly he was serious, alert; he was up the stairs three at a time, and a second later they were both in Sally's room.

Somehow, Daphne had known what she would see. The tumbled bed, the scattering of toys and papers on the floor round it; and that was all. Sally was gone.

Tim's voice was hoarse and strange.

"She must have got her downstairs," he said; but Daphne could tell that he knew as well as she did that there was no one anywhere in that silent house. Her attention was riveted by the papers scattered on the bed and over the floor; and as she stepped nearer she could see that they were from Mrs Hahn's writing pad. Sheet after sheet of them, all with pictures drawn on them. Pictures of hens. Hens with big eyes; hens with huge, fantastic eyes; hens with eyes so grotesque that it was hard to conceive of a sane adult mind having perpetrated them.

How had the woman known? By what loathsome subterranean channel of the mind could she have found out the child's secret terror and tormented her thus before—

Before what?

It was the telephone shrilling through the house that roused her from her paralysis; but Tim reached it before she did.

"Yes," he was saying. "What? St Luke's Hospital? Yes. Yes, of course. No, we had no idea."

Daphne leaned close in time to hear the bland professional voice the other end saying:

"... Acute appendicitis, she has had the operation, and everything is going very well. And may I say you were extremely fortunate to have such a sensible, quick-witted woman in charge of the little girl. Anyone less experienced would never have realized how seriously ill she was. Sometimes, you know, with young children, you don't get severe pain with it at all—it can be most misleading.

There can be a number of mild attacks—just waking at night, or nightmares—perhaps a little sickness—and then —well—the last attack. I must say again how *very* fortunate it was that you had a woman of such experience and presence of mind. She is with us now at the hospital. You would like to speak to her, I expect."

How reassuring the gruff foreign voice sounded to Daphne now; how full of kindliness and hard-won wisdom.

"She cry, the little one, I go to her. She is hot, she cries of bird with great eyes, of great hen. She is sick, and I know it is something with her stomach, something bad. I call the doctor, and while we wait for the doctor I try to take her fear away of the great hen, of the great eyes. I draw funny pictures of hen, and she laugh. She draw in funny eyes. I draw more funny hens, she draw in more funny eyes, we laugh together about funny hen with funny eyes ... I think she will be no more frightened of hens and eyes...."

"And actually," remarked Tim, much later in that eventful night, "the German for 'Hen' isn't 'Hahn' at all. It's 'Huhn'."

THE HATED HOUSE

Now THAT SHE had it to herself, Lorna felt that she could almost enjoy hating her home so much. She flung her school coat and beret on to the sofa, dumped her satchel down in the middle of the floor, and watched with satisfaction as the books and papers spilled out over her mother's spotless, well-vacuumed carpet. It was nice to be able to mess it up like that, without risk of reprimand. She gazed round the neat, firelit room with contempt. Hideous ornaments—houseplants, bric-à-brac of all kinds; and on either side of the fire those two neat, well upholstered armchairs were drawn up, for all the world as if a happily married couple habitually sat in them; a contented couple, smiling at each other across the hearth; not a couple like Lorna's parents, wrangling, bickering, squabbling, the long evenings filled with temper or with tears....

With slatternly, spread-eagled violence, Lorna flung herself into the nearest of the two chairs, sending it skidding and scratching under her weight across the polished wood surround.

That was better! Lorna spread out the length of her

THE HATED HOUSE

legs untidily, in the luxurious abandonment of solitude: real, reliable, long-term solitude, a whole glorious evening of it, and a whole night to follow!

Such a fuss there had been, about this simple business of leaving her alone in the house for a night! Just as if she had been a baby, instead of a young woman of nearly sixteen!

"Be sure you bolt all the doors," her mother had said, not once but fifty times: "Be sure you put the guard in front of the fire before you go to bed.... Be sure you turn off the oven.... Be sure you don't answer the door to anyone you don't know.... Remember you can always go in to the Holdens if you feel in the least bit nervous...."

Go in to the Holdens, indeed! Lorna would have died—yes, she would willingly have lain right here on the carpet with her throat cut—before she would run for help to that dreary Holden woman, both boring and sly, chatter chatter over the wall to Mummy about the problems of teenage daughters. Ugh!

Ah, but this was the life! Lorna slid yet deeper and more luxuriously into the cushioned depths of the chair. Tea when she liked; supper when she liked; homework when she liked; music when she liked. Lorna's eyes turned with lazy anticipation towards the pile of pop records stacked under the record player. Ah, the fuss there usually was over those records, with Mummy twittering in and out, trying to stop Daddy being annoyed by them.... "Can't you turn it down lower, dear?... Can't you play them in the afternoons when Daddy's not here? You know how it annoys him."

What Mummy didn't realize was that actually it was

quite fun annoying Daddy—a real roaring bellowing row instead of all these anxious twitterings! And afterwards Daddy would go on yelling at Mummy for hours, long after the records were finished and done with. And then next day Mummy would scuttle about with red eyes, polishing things, as if a tidy polished house was some sort of protection against quarrelling! Honestly, *adults!* That's why I hate the smell of polish, thought Lorna, deliberately jolting the chair on its rusty castors back and forth across the polished boards, making deep dents and scratches in the wood. It's misery-polish that Mummy puts on everything, it's dishonesty-polish, trying to make this look like a happy home when it isn't! It's because she's too cowardly, too much of a doormat, to stand up to Daddy's tempers, so she tidies the house instead.... I bet she's tidied the kitchen even better than usual today, just because she's nervous about leaving me alone! She thinks tidiness is a substitute for everything! Stirred by a flicker of resentful curiosity, and also by a mounting interest in the thought of tea, Lorna dragged herself from her luxurious position, and went to the kitchen to investigate.

Yes, it was immaculate. Every surface scrubbed and shining; a delicious little dish of cold chicken and salad all ready for Lorna's supper; and for her tea—just look! a big, expensive, once-in-a-lifetime meringue, bursting with cream! A *treat!* Another of Mummy's pathetic attempts to provide Lorna with at least the shell of a happy home! Irritation fought in Lorna with eager appetite. Does she think I'm a baby, or something, who needs to be consoled for its Mummy being away? I *love* Mummy

THE HATED HOUSE

being away! I love it! I love it!—and with each "love" her teeth sank deeper into the rare, luscious thing; the cream spurted with bounteous prodigality across her cheeks, and she didn't even have to wipe them, because she was alone. Alone, alone, alone: the nearest thing to Paradise.

Outside, the spring evening was fading. The sob and thrum of Lorna's favourite records mingled first with a pink sunset light in the pale room; then with a pearly, silvery greyness against which the firelight glowed ever more orange and alive; and at last, curtains drawn, lamps switched on, coal piled recklessly into a roaring blaze, it was night; and still the records played on, over and over again. It was too lovely a time, this time of firelight and perfect solitude, to waste on anything less beautiful than the music which her parents hated so.

It was nearly nine o'clock when the telephone began to ring. It began just as Lorna had settled herself cosily by the fire with her tray of chicken salad, new rolls, and a huge mug of boiling hot, sweet black coffee, whose deliciousness was enhanced by the fact that Mummy would have said: Don't have it black, dear, not at this time of night, it'll keep you awake.

Damn! she thought, setting down the mug just in the middle of the first glorious sip. Damn! and then: Why don't I just not answer it? Why don't I ignore it? I bet it'll just be Mummy, fussing about something. Yes, driving along those monotonous miles of motorway, she'll have been thinking up some new things to fuss about: Have I latched the kitchen window? Have I brought the milk in off the step? Will I be sure and shut the spare room window if it rains? Fuss, fuss, fuss, an expensive long-distance fuss from a roadside callbox.... I *won't* answer, why should I? I'll just let it ring, serve her right, teach her a lesson, show her I'm not a baby.... Defiantly, Lorna raised the mug to her lips once more, and calmly, leisurely, she resumed her sipping.

But how the telephone kept on! It was irritating, it was spoiling this solitary, delightful meal which she had planned to savour to the full. She laid down her knife and fork restlessly. Weren't they *ever* going to ring off? How long *do* people go on ringing before they finally give up? ... and just then, at last, with a despairing little hiccup, the telephone ceased ringing.

Silence swung back into the room, and flooded Lorna with relief. She picked up her knife and fork once more, and prepared to recapture her interrupted bliss. Having a meal alone by the fire like this; *Alone!* The joy of it! No table-manners. No conversation. Just peace, delicious peace.

But somehow it had all been spoiled. The slow, savoury mouthfuls tasted of almost nothing now; the new, favourite magazine propped against the coffee-pot could not hold her attention; and she was conscious of an odd tenseness, a waiting, listening unease in every nerve. She finished the meal without enjoyment, and as she carried the tray out to the kitchen the telephone began again.

The shock was somehow extraordinary. Almost dropping the tray on to the kitchen table, Lorna turned and ran headlong back into the sitting-room slamming the door behind her as if that would somehow protect her from the imperious, nagging summons. All her sense of guilt and unease at not having answered before seemed to make it doubly impossible to answer now; and the longer she let it ring, the more impossible it became. Why should anybody ring so long, and so persistently? If it was Mummy, then surely she would have assumed by now that Lorna had gone in to the Holdens? Who else could it be who would ring, and ring, and ring like this? Surely no one goes on ringing a number *for ever*? Oh, please God, make it stop!

And at last, of course, it did stop; and again the silence filled her ears in a great flood, but this time there was no relief in it. She felt herself so tense, so tightly listening, it was almost as if she knew, deep in her knotted stomach, just what was going to happen next.

It was a light, a very light footstep on the garden path that next caught at her hearing; lightly up the steps, and then a fumbling at the front door. Not a knock; not a ring; just a fumbling, as of someone trying to unlock the door; someone too weak, or too blind, to turn the key.

"Be sure you bolt all the doors...." In her head Lorna seemed to hear these boring, familiar instructions not for the fiftieth time, but for the first.... "Be sure you latch the kitchen window.... Don't answer the door to anyone you don't know...."

Lorna tiptoed out into the hall, and for a few moments she fancied that she must have imagined the sounds, for all was quiet. No shadowy silhouette could be seen looming against the frosted panels of the door, palely glittering in the light of the street lamp. But even as she stood there, the flap of the letter-box began to stir, slowly. Lorna was looking into an eye.

A single eye, of course, as it would be if anyone is peering through a letter-box; and yet, irrationally, it was this singleness that shocked most, carrying one back, in an instant, beyond the civilized centuries, right back to the Cyclops, to the mad, mythical beginnings of mankind. Lorna began to scream.

"Don't be frightened," came a voice from outside—a young voice, Lorna registered with gasping thankfulness and surprise. Why, it was a *girl's* voice: a girl no older than herself by the sound of it! "Don't be frightened, Lorna—but do please let me in!"

Reassured completely by the sound of her own name, Lorna ran to the door and flung it open.

"Oh, you *did* give me a fright—" she was beginning, but then stopped, puzzled. For though the girl standing there looked vaguely familiar, and was roughly her own age, Lorna did not know her. She had taken for granted, when she heard herself addressed by name, that she would be bound to recognize the speaker.

"Hallo! I—that is, I'm awfully sorry, I'm sure I ought to know you—?" she began uncertainly.

"It's all right; I didn't think you would recognize me at once," answered the girl, stepping confidently into the hall, and looking round her. "I hope you don't mind my coming out of the blue like this; but I used to live here, you see."

She was a forceful looking girl, Lorna could see now, standing there under the hall light; with strong black hair springing from a high, very white forehead, and her eyes were dark, and snapping bright; as if, thought Lorna, she had a quick temper and a quick wit, and very much a will of her own.

"Oh, I see." Lorna tried to collect her wits. This must be the daughter of the family who had lived here before Lorna's family had moved in, seven or eight years ago. "Oh, I see— Fancy you remembering my name! Do come in—I expect you'd like to look at everything, see how it's changed since you were here." Already she felt that she was going to like this girl, who was looking round with such bright interest, and seemed so friendly. "I'll show you my room first, shall I; I wonder if it was the same one you had? It's the little back one that looks out on the garden."

By the time they had explored the house, Lorna felt as if she and this other girl had known each other for years. They seemed to have so much the same tastes, the same loves and hates; and as they sat over the fire afterwards, with a newly made pot of coffee between them, Lorna found herself confiding in her new friend all her troubles: Daddy's tempers; Mummy's doormat submission to him, her anxious, fussy housekeeping.

"I wouldn't mind," she explained, "if Mummy was *really* a houseproud sort of person—if she really got any pleasure out of making the house look nice. But she doesn't. She does it in a desperate sort of way. She clutters everything up with flowers, and hideous ornaments—"

"—as if it was a substitute for making you and your father happy, you mean?" put in the other girl quickly. "You mean, since she can't give you a happy home, she's determined to give you a neat, clean one, full of things?"

"That's it! That's it exactly!" cried Lorna. "How well you understand! But why such *ugly* things?" Her eyes swept the mantelpiece and the crowded corner cupboard. "It's as if she collected ugly things on purpose."

"I don't think so," said the other girl quickly, glancing rapidly round the room. "They're not actually ugly, you know—not each of them taken singly. It's just that nobody loves them—your mother and father never chose any of them together, in a little dark shop, on holiday when they were enjoying themselves. I expect your mother bought them pretending it was like that when it wasn't."

"Why, yes! I expect she did! That would be exactly like her!" cried Lorna, enchanted. Never had she found anyone before who could understand the way this girl understood. "That's why I hate them so—"

"So let's smash them," said the other girl, in the same quiet, thoughtful tones. "Let's bash them to pieces on the marble fireplace there. Think how they'd crash and shatter!" There was a strange gleam in her dark eyes, and Lorna stared at her, for the first time uneasy. But she was joking—of course she was.

"Wouldn't I just love to!" Lorna gave a little laugh appropriate to such nonsense. "Have some more coffee?"

"No. I mean it. Let's! You hate them—you are right to hate them. Hateful things should be s-s-s-smashed!" And snatching a china shepherdess from the mantelpiece, the girl flung it with all her force into the grate.

The splintering, shocking, unimaginable crash shocked Lorna speechless. "Stop!" she tried to cry as a teapot and two vases burst like spray across the hearthrug; and then, even as she gasped out her protests, something extraordinary began to seep into her soul. Shock, yes; but what was this joy, this exultation, this long pent-up anger, as crash followed crash and splinters of china rebounded across the room like hail?

"Smash them! Smash them!" the girl was crying, her dark face alight with extraordinary joy. "Rip up the cushions! Tear down the curtains—they were sewn in misery, not in love, every stitch was stitched in misery!" With a great rending, ripping sigh, the curtains huddled to the floor; and by now both girls were upon them, ripping, tearing. A madness not her own was in Lorna now, and she too was tearing, smashing, hurling, in an ecstasy of shared destruction such as she had never dreamed.

Dreamed? *Was* she dreaming, then? Was this the telephone waking her, ringing, ringing, ringing across the devastated room? This time, Lorna ran instantly to answer, snatched it from its hook and waited.

Yes. Yes, this was the home of Mrs Mary Webster. Yes, I'm her daughter. No, I'm afraid my father is not in. You rang several times before? Oh. Yes what is it? What is it?

An accident. My dear, I'm very, very sorry to have to tell you ... an accident ... your mother. Yes. Your mother ... a lorry out of a side road ... it must have been instantaneous.... And a lot more, kindly, helpful, sympathetic, kind people on their way to Lorna right now. Lorna couldn't really take it in.

She was not surprised, when she went slowly back to the sitting-room, to find that her new friend was gone. She had known that she would be gone, for she knew, now, who it must have been. For who else was there who could have hated the room as Lorna hated it, and would have come back, at the last, to destroy it?

And, after all, the destruction was not so very great; for a ghost, even using all its strength, is not strong as a living person is strong. A few things were broken, the curtains crumpled and awry; and as Lorna sat down among the mussed cushions she was crying: crying with happiness because she and her mother—her real mother, the one hidden beneath the doormat exterior for all these years—had understood each other at the last.

ANGEL-FACE

"But there are angels, Mummy. Miss Sowerby says there are. She says they have wings, too, and bright lights round their heads. *Ever* so bright! As bright as the headlamps of Daddy's car, Miss Sowerby says!"

I sighed. Bother Miss Sowerby! And bother Daddy, too, for that matter!—if Philip wanted his son to be brought up in his own humanist-rationalist opinions, then where was the sense in sending him to an old-fashioned little village school, where the last of the world's Miss Sowerby's are bound to be still quietly flourishing? But of course I would never argue about it: right from the moment of marrying him, I had resolved never to argue with Philip about Simon's upbringing. The important things for a six-year-old—or so I reasoned—were consistency—continuity—stability. The task of a new stepmother, it seemed to me, was to keep things going for the child as nearly as possible as they had always been. No change was as important as *no change*, if you see what I mean; and this had been my policy throughout these first, difficult months.

And difficult, indeed, they had been. It would have

been easier if Simon had been, quite simply, a more attractive child: if he had been a bouncing, handsome, extrovert little boy, who could be made happy by treats, and toys, and ice-cream: a little boy with muddy knees and football boots and lots of noisy little friends. I had come into my marriage all set to be tolerant about that sort of thing; to smile as I patched torn dungarees, swept mud off the carpets, and accustomed my ears to the clatter and yells of Cowboys and Indians up and down the stairs and in and out of the back door.

But Simon isn't like that at all, I am sorry to say. He is a pale, mopish little creature, who reads a lot (yes, at six he reads voraciously, fluent as an adult), and his eyes are always red-rimmed, sometimes from eyestrain, sometimes, I suppose, from crying. Personally, I think he oughtn't to be *allowed* to read so much; but, as I say, I never interfere; I keep my opinions to myself. If he was *my* child—that is to say, if I was his real own mother, and didn't have to be so careful all the time not to upset him—I would *insist* on him going out more, and leading a more active life. I would take him for long walks whether he liked it or not; I would invite little boys to tea myself, and make him play with them. I just couldn't endure to see a son of *mine* so pallid, and unsociable, and full of fancies. But since he *isn't* my son, and since Philip seems to see nothing amiss, I let him go his own way, and just try to be very, very kind to him. I think I can honestly say that in all these months I have never once slapped him, or even raised my voice in anger. All my friends say it's marvellous, how patient I am with him, even when he is at his most whiny and

ANGEL-FACE

tiresome; and I am glad to be told this, because, believe me, I don't always *feel* patient! There are times, there really are, when Simon would try the patience of an angel, particularly when he is in one of his argumentative moods. Of course, I know that six-year-olds are always argumentative—I'm not complaining of that—it's right and natural that they should be. But with Simon it's different. With him it's not the normal, aggressive, "I'm right and you're wrong!" sort of attitude, that is typical of bright little boys. On the contrary, it's as if he doesn't *want* you to be wrong—is afraid of it, somehow—and he's all twisted up with anxiety to put you right.

Like this angel business, for instance. They have Religious Instruction on Friday afternoons, and it seems that on this particular Friday Miss Sowerby had seen fit to stuff the kids' heads with even more fairy-tale nonsense than usually goes under the heading of "Religion". Of course, it should all have slid off him like water off a duck's back as soon as the lesson was over—that's what happens with any normal child. But Simon is not like that. Perhaps for the very reason that he has been brought up in an atheistic household, all this religious claptrap actually *means* something to him. He actually *listens*, I mean, and thinks he is learning some new and extraordinary fact about the world: a child from an ordinary religious home would never dream of paying that much attention.

And so then, of course, being Simon, he comes home all het-up and anxious about it, and lets his tea grow cold, and the nice hot-buttered toast that I always have ready for him on winter afternoons congeals on his plate, while he worries at the topic like a terrier with a bone.

"But Mummy, they've got great *wings*, Miss Sowerby says, as—as big as right across this room! That's how big they'd have to be, to fly an angel right off the floor!"

His eyes were round with awe as they took in the size of our sitting-room and visualized the wing-span that would reach from wall to wall. This solemn, objective assessment of such a piece of fairy-tale rubbish made me want to laugh; but of course I was careful not to do so; one should never laugh at a child.

"No, Simon," I said gently. "You've got the wrong idea. Miss Sowerby didn't mean there really *are* such things as angels (she did, of course, the silly cow, but what else could I say?). She just meant that—well—that you can *imagine* such creatures, as symbols of goodness. You know what a 'symbol' is?"

He did, of course. Simon always knows the meanings of words. I sometimes think he'd be a more lovable child if he didn't—and a happier one, too. Already that irritating little nervous pucker was coming and going on his forehead as he talked—a sure sign that he was working himself up into one of his states. I don't ever let him see that it irritates me, of course, because I know he can't help it. So I just smiled at him reassuringly and said: "That's all angels are, Simon, just a fanciful way of talking about goodness! You mustn't start thinking about them as if they were *real*."

But Simon wouldn't let it go—he never will. He gets his nerves wound round something, like a spider's web round a fly, and there is nothing you can do.

"No," he said, with his own special air of anxiety-ridden obstinacy. "That isn't what Miss Sowerby meant. She meant there *are* angels. She says you can see them sometimes. People who are very, very good, *they* can see them, she says. Am *I* very, very good, Mummy?"

I sighed. I could see that it was hopeless.

"Of course you are, Simon, dear," I said brightly—and I wasn't lying, either. He *is* a good little boy—too good. Naughty little boys are more lovable, to my way of thinking.

"*Of course* you're good!" I repeated reassuringly. "Very, very good! We'll tell Daddy how good you've been, shall we, when he comes in?"

"No!" Astonishingly, the little pallid face was puckered almost into tears, and I was filled with a familiar, baffled irritation. Here I was, trying my hardest to be nice to him, to show approval, and all he could do was to look as if I'd kicked him! "No, don't tell Daddy that!" he begged, clutching at my sleeve with his weak, damp little fingers. "Please don't tell Daddy I'm good! Please, Mummy!"

When you can't understand, the thing to do is to smile, and be very, very kind. So I patted the perverse little creature's head—his hair is always a little greasy, and unpleasant to the touch, however often I wash it—I smiled my brightest, and suggested a game of draughts before bedtime. It's a boring game, made even more boring for me by the fact that I always play so as to let Simon win; but it's the sort of sedentary game that seems to suit him, and as I'm only playing for his sake anyway, it doesn't matter that I'm bored.

Well, his bedtime came at last, and he went off meekly

enough and Philip came in, and we had dinner; and it wasn't until we were sitting over the fire drinking our coffee that a sudden shriek of "Mummy! Mummy!" sent me racing up the stairs.

Believe it or not, it was the angels again! Apparently that fool of a Miss Sowerby had told the kids that if they were good children an angel would watch over them at night while they slept! And Simon—trust him!— had managed to convert this hackneyed drivel into a vision of terror! It seemed that he had had a dream— or had let his imagination run riot in the darkness, there was no way of telling which—but anyway, he had opened his eyes and fancied he saw a circle of light in the half-open doorway, and had heard a rustle of wings.

"It was coming up the stairs, Mummy!" he gasped, half in and half out of his nightmare; "It was coming in the door! It was all bright, like a headlamp, and I could hear its wings rustling!"

I soothed him as best I could; and then Philip came up and talked to him too, telling him all the comforting Rationalist doctrines about things not being real unless scientists have measured them and taken photographs of them and that sort of thing; and gradually Simon became calmer, and presently he fell asleep, a secure, cared-for little boy, with one of his parents on each side of his bed, just as it should be.

The rightness of this picture struck both of us; and when we got down to the sitting-room, Philip put his arms around me and told me how marvellous I was with Simon. "He's *ours* now, isn't he?" he said, covering my face with kisses. "Not just *mine*. *Our* son! And did you notice how he called 'Mummy!' tonight? Not 'Daddy!'? It's *you* he wants now when he's frightened. He has really accepted you at last!"

It was true; it really was a step forward. At the beginning, Simon had balked at calling me "Mummy"—it almost seemed that he must still remember something of his real mother, who had died when he was three. We hadn't forced him, of course—that would have been wrong. We had simply and firmly referred to me as "Mummy"—Philip in talking of me in his presence and I in referring to myself, and at last Simon had got used to it. And now, here he was calling to "Mummy!" for comfort in the night! It was one of my moments of triumph.

But I have to admit that as night followed night, this sense of triumph began to wear a little thin. Because it turned out that Simon's nightmare that evening—or hysterical fancy, or whatever it was—was not just an isolated little episode, to be laughed off and forgotten; it was the beginning of a long and worrying obsession which was to try my patience to the limit. At first it was just in the evenings. Around nine o'clock, just as it had been the first time, the cry "Mummy! Mummy!" would ring down the stairs; and I would have to leave my coffee, or my book, and run up to calm him down. Over and over again, evening after evening, I found myself mouthing the same soothing rigmarole: "But Simon, dear, there *can't* be such things as angels, because...." "No, dear, there *wasn't* an angel standing by your bed when I came in...." "No, dear, it *isn't* true that anyone has ever seen one, it's just a story.... No, I *can't* hear a rustling sound, only the wind in the trees; and no, that light *isn't* coming from the stairs, it's only the moon outside the window ... and no, it *isn't* getting brighter, of course it isn't...."

Each night it seemed to take longer before he settled down; each night I had a harder struggle to hide my impatience and irritation. And my scorn, too, really; a boy, even a *little* boy, should surely have more pride than to give way so helplessly to such idle fancies? Not that I ever suggested such a thing to the child, or urged him to be "a brave boy", as I would have done if he had been *my* son, and I had needed to be proud of him. I knew, you see, that he couldn't help it, he'd been born with these morbid and cowardly tendencies, and all one could do was to be sorry for him, not angry or reproachful. Anger, or any sort of disapproval, would only have made him worse, the poor spiritless little thing.

But it *was* a strain, and I don't mind admitting it; and instead of getting better as the days went by it got worse. Presently he began waking up in the night too, as well as in the evenings. I would have to drag myself from my bed and go in to him at one in the morning, or two, or three. Shivering in my dressing-gown, half dead with drowsiness, I would stand at his bedside and recite the familiar sentences almost in my sleep.... "No, Simon, dear, there *can't* be such things as angels.... No, there *isn't* a rustling noise coming up the stairs...."

Sometimes, to give me a rest, Philip would go to him instead of me; but all that happened then was that Simon would go on crying "Mummy! Mummy!" until finally

I had to go. Quite often, actually, he would do the same with me—I mean, he would go on crying "Mummy! Mummy!" after I was already there, and doing my best to soothe him! It was puzzling, this: but Simon *is* a puzzling child, as I am sure I have made clear by now.

Time went by, and my nights grew ever more hideous with weariness and broken sleep; and now Simon's obsession began to spill over into the daytime as well. He began searching our bookshelves for references to angels, and one evening, coming on a picture of an angel in some book or other—a book on medieval history, I think it was—he said something so odd that it really gave me quite a shock.

"Look, Mummy!" he exclaimed, bringing the book over to me "Look, this one hasn't got a beak!"

"A beak?" I said, mystified; and it turned out—would you believe it?—that he had all this time been imagining that angels had *beaks*! Because they had wings—that was the connection in his mind—and he'd pictured their beaks as huge and curved, like a vulture's. He thought they had vulture's eyes, too—hooded eyes, peering out from among their haloes and gauzy draperies and whatnot! Oh, and claws, too, where their hands should be. Can you credit it? An intelligent child of nearly seven!

Well, you might suppose—you who don't know our Simon—you might suppose that the discovery that angels don't have beaks and claws would have dispelled the nightmares. But Oh, no! He decided—with his usual obstinacy—that the picture was *wrong*!—just as he'd decided that *we* were wrong in saying there weren't such things as angels at all. It was no use arguing—it never is, with him: and, to be fair, I have to admit that people who say there aren't such things as angels are on rather shaky ground when they start saying also that angels haven't got beaks.

So the nightmares continued; and the crying out in the night; and the daytime obsession grew, if anything, worse. He began about this time to make dreary little attempts to be naughty—Miss Sowerby's fatuous assertion that it was the "very, very good" children who were liable to see angels at their bedside—this seemed to be fixed in his mind for ever, and nothing would dislodge it. So he took the (admittedly logical) course of trying to be naughty. I say "trying", because he was far too timid and anxious a child ever to bring it off. He would take a cup, sometimes, or a saucer, and tap it feebly against the kitchen floor trying to break it—but not daring, you understand, *really* to break it, by banging really hard. Or he would play truant from school—for five minutes, hanging about in the lane—and then run in, crying, and not even late for prayers!

And still—though I say it myself—I kept my temper with him. Philip said I was marvellous, an angel of patience; it was only his praise and encouragement that made it possible for me to carry on, I feel sure of that. Thanks to him, I stuck it out, night after night, shivering at Simon's bedside, swallowing down my impatience and resentment; never letting it show in my voice, or in my face, or in the gentle touch of my hand as I stroked his hot little forehead and his horrid, greasy hair.

One night, after Simon had called me up three times, it seemed silly to go to bed again; he would only call me up again. So I went downstairs and sat by the dead fire, with my head in my hands, and my dressing-gown pulled tight around me against the cold. My head drooped with weariness, my eyelids were heavy like two stones; and upstairs—asleep, I hoped—lay the little slave-driver who had established the right to keep me from my rest for ever. The sickly, neurotic little beast: the morbid, loathsome little milksop: the apple of his father's eye....

"Mummy! Mummy!"

The cry woke me: that's how I knew that I had been asleep. They were only dreams, then, those dark, unruly thoughts, which ordinarily I would never think. I still seemed to be half-dreaming as I stumbled up the stairs; my eyes seemed dazzled, as if by a great light; and yet everything was in darkness. My dressing-gown had grown longer, somehow, and heavier; it rustled stiffly behind me, catching softly on the steps of the stairs as I went up and up.

"Mummy! Mummy!" Yet more urgent came the cry. "I'm coming!" I called in answer, and began to summon up the soothing, comforting smile which I always try to force on to my face for Simon.

But why wouldn't the smile come? What was this stiffness where my lips should be? I tried to open my mouth to call out again; but it was not my mouth that opened; it was a great beak, jutting out of my face, cruel and curved like a bird of prey; and I knew now that my eyelids, so heavy with lack of sleep, were heavy and hooded, above my yellow vulture's eyes. My robes were gauzy and beautiful, floating round me like a mist, and my great wings quivered restlessly, ready for flight. The dazzle in my eyes grew brighter, and now I knew that it came from within; my beaked face was blazing, bright as the headlights on Daddy's car, and in that awful radiance I could see that my hands had become claws, yellow and crooked as they clutched the banisters. They looked eager, somehow, as they pulled me upwards and onwards, compensating for my useless clawed feet that clattered and slithered on the polished stairs.

"Mummy! Mummy!"

"I'm coming, dear, I'm coming!" I called—but how harsh and eerie the words sounded as the beak mouthed them, clumsily: so I tried again.

"I'm coming!" I squawked; and, with a final clumsy spurt I slithered and rattled on my claws across the landing. With a rustle of half-raised wings, I swooped into Simon's darkened room, and leaned over his little bed, just as I always do, to comfort him.

THE FATED INTERVIEW

EVER SINCE SHE had started the new job, Lydia had suffered from these awful dreams. No, not really dreams, for even now she was not really asleep—Lydia turned her throbbing head yet again on the pillow, seeking a coolness, a relaxation which was nowhere; never to be found again.

No, she was not asleep, and these whirling, compulsive visions were not dreams, but just the fevered, obsessional thinking of insomnia, hammering on and on, hour after hour, giving her no rest....

"Excuse me, we are doing a survey of hair colorants; I wonder if I might ask you a few questions...?"

"Excuse me, do you mind telling me how often you watch television?... Very interesting, fairly interesting, rather uninteresting, very uninteresting...?"—the word "interesting" seemed to go round and round under her eyelids, like the lettering on a spinning coin— "And, lastly, I wonder if you'd mind telling me which of these age-groups you belong to—35-44, 45-64...?"

One after another the pursed-up disapproving faces of the respondents loomed out of the darkness:

"... Well, *really*! Don't you think it's a little impertinent, asking these sort of personal questions of a complete stranger?"

"I'm sorry, I really haven't the time for this sort of thing...."

"I'm sorry, but I'm afraid I can't go on answering these questions. I've already told you that I don't smoke, so how *can* I tell you what I think of your wretched brand?"

And then the face of Lydia's supervisor flashed on the awful inner screen: "I'm sorry, Miss Steele, I'm afraid we can't accept an incomplete interview like this. It was explained quite clearly at the Briefing on Monday that non-smokers as well as smokers must answer *all* the questions. What, you can't *make* them answer? But my dear woman, it's your *job* to make them answer. That's what we pay you for. The *other* interviewers manage it!"

Lydia pushed the stifling blankets away from her face, and stared up into the darkness. The *Other* Interviewers! The Enemy! Smart, calm, and unafraid, they always managed everything. With bright, impervious, battering-ram tenacity they pushed ahead with page after page of questions whose repetitive idiocy often made Lydia want to crawl out of sight down the nearest manhole.

How did they do it? Most of them, of course, were younger than Lydia: perhaps the brash cheekiness of youth was what was needed? Or was it perhaps not so much that they were young as they were married? One and all, they exuded the supreme, impenetrable confidence of the woman who is wanted: the woman who has someone to go home to. As Lydia had once had. In the days when her life was a real life; in the days before she had had to give up her well-paid, interesting job at the advertising agency, and had moved into this dreadful, sunless bed-sittingroom.

She sometimes wondered if the heartbreak would have been less if she had stayed to endure it in her well-paid job, weeping the weekends away in her expensive, pretty flat, with the familiar fitted carpet and the sun streaming in at the big windows? But no—it would have been impossible. Even if she had known how difficult it would be, for a woman of her age, to get another job of the same sort; even if she had known that she would be reduced to this awful Market Research work in order to stay alive—even if she had known all this in advance, she still could not have contemplated staying on in the same firm as Clive, now that he had left her. Left her after fifteen years. Left her just when his divorce had at long last come through, and he was free to marry her. The moment for which they had—apparently—been waiting all those long years, during which he had seemed to love her so faithfully. Seemed? No, he *had* loved her, Lydia felt sure of it: had loved her truly, with all the feeble strength of his selfish, vacillating soul.

Oh yes, she had not been blind to his faults; how could she be, after fifteen years? But she had loved him in spite of them—or was it even because of them? For what man is so easy to please as the selfish man—the man who can be caught and held by such simple things as good cooking, by shameless flattery, and by being given his own way about absolutely everything? can be held, that is, so long as no one else comes along who can cook even better, can cosset even more skilfully, can give him his own way on even more occasions?

Was Paula such a person? Lydia knew—had wanted to know—nothing about the girl except her name; but round this name her imagination had woven a figure blonde and beautiful, of infinite sweetness and unselfishness—a figure which was also, and above all, *young*. Young, that was it. The familiar, angry tears pricked into Lydia's eyes as she faced yet again the cruel fact that this was the one thing she could no longer give to Clive. She, who through all the long years had given him everything, could no longer give him youth.

Somehow, as she lay there, the anger, the bitterness and the grinding jealousy all combined together to produce a misery so clear-cut as to be a sort of peace: the whirling panorama of questionnaires and faces ... faces and questionnaires ... began to blur, and at last, just as the dawn was beginning to lighten in the blank square of the window, Lydia fell asleep.

She woke late, to the accusing sound of busy, midmorning traffic; and even though no gleam of sunlight ever reached this horrid little north room she could sense that the morning sun was already high.

Nearly eleven! Too late, already, to catch the mothers depositing their offspring at the gates of the primary school—always a good hunting ground for D-class F's aged 25-34. Already, after only six weeks of this work, Lydia found herself classifying her fellow-beings in these sort of terms. She knew that this was going to be a dreadful day, she was coming to the end of her quota, so that only special categories of people would do. You had to size up each victim before you pounced: is he over 45? Is he an AB—a doctor, or a barrister, or something like that? Or is he a schoolteacher, a mere C?

The AB men were the worst. By teatime, Lydia was still short of three of them, all to be between the ages of 45 and 64. How could one possibly expect three such exalted beings to be loafing about the Kilburn High Road at four o'clock on a Wednesday afternoon? She was hot; she was exhausted; her feet seemed to be swelling out of her shoes; and she had just had four failures in succession —three polite but icy refusals, and one merry little man in a deceptively well-cut suit, who was very ready to be interviewed but who proved to be an out-and-out unmistakeable D.

Lydia clenched her teeth, summoned up her last shreds of courage, and stepped up to yet another possibility— a tall greying man who was staring abstractedly into the window of a camera shop.

"Excuse me—" the words came parched and parrotlike from her lips after the long, desperate day. "Excuse me, we are doing a survey on smoking habits, and—"

The grey face under the grey hair swivelled slowly round, and with sick, accustomed dread Lydia saw in it the familiar icy, aristocratic surprise.

"I *beg* your pardon?" came the cool, expected snub. "No, not today, thank you," and as he moved away, stiff with righteous affront, Lydia tried to hunch herself into invisibility in the nearest doorway, scarlet with familiar shame.

"Were you looking for an AB, male, over 45?"

The smooth pleasant voice, full of friendly interest,

was so astonishing after the disheartening, day-long battle, that at first Lydia could only stare helplessly into the bronzed weatherbeaten face that smiled lazily down at her. She felt vaguely that he reminded her of someone, but she did not pursue the thought: *who* he was, was not important; what *was* important was that he was about 55, and an undoubted A. He was well-dressed, he spoke with a cultivated voice—he could be exactly right. So right that Lydia, dazed and exhausted, thought for a moment that she must be dreaming.

"Oh *yes!*" she cried. "Are you—could I—? But how do you know—about my quota, I mean, and the AB's...?" her voice trailed away in confusion, and her companion laughed and patted her arm.

"I've been watching you for quite a while," he admitted. "I could see you were having a bad day. I used to be involved in these market research things myself once upon a time, so I know what it's like. Now then. What is it? Margarine? Leisure activities? Brands of toothpaste? Fire away!"

He answered everything beautifully. He *was* a smoker; he had heard of all the brands of cigarette that Lydia had to ask him about, and he could also say instantly and without any fuss whether things were very important, rather important or not important at all to him, and whether they were less important, very much less important, or only rather less important than other things. He did not get bored or irritated with the monotonous triviality of the questions, and when it came to the final question—the open ended one, where he had to say exactly how he felt about cigarette smoking, and Lydia had to write it down word for word, he seemed to consider the question with real interest.

"I suppose, for me," he said thoughtfully, "smoking is a sort of tranquillizer. I wasn't always a smoker, you know. I began to smoke at a time when I was young, and very, very unhappy—it seemed to take my mind off the miserable thoughts—the kind of thoughts one thinks when one is young. You know the sort of thing— Life has no more meaning? I've lost everything that made living worth while—all I want is to make an end to it all."

He stopped, letting Lydia's flying biro catch up with him—shorthand was not allowed in this job, you had to write out everything in full, on the spot, that was one of the strictest regulations. Lydia wondered what she should do if his reminiscences should overrun the space allotted for this last question; but rather to her surprise his confidences seemed to stop short at this point.

"Is that all?" she asked—against the rules, this, but somehow she had thought she was about to hear quite a long story. Tiresome in a way, when respondents embarked on the long story of their life, but also interesting.

"That's all," he said, rather shortly: and then: "Don't you want my name and address? So that they can check up on you, make sure you didn't make it up?"

"You *are* well up in it all, aren't you?" laughed Lydia. "Yes, we do need it: would you mind—?" She looked up at him enquiringly, biro poised: but instead of answering, he reached out his hand.

"You'd better let me write it in myself," he said. "My name's impossible to spell at first hearing, and my address is almost as bad."

Lydia handed him the form and the biro, and heaved a great sigh of relief. Not only was another questionnaire solidly filled in, but so pleasant and friendly an encounter would boost her morale tremendously for tackling the next comers.

And only then did she realize that her companion had turned sharply on his heel and was walking away. Walking swiftly—hurrying, darting away into the crowd!

For a couple of seconds astonishment held her absolutely motionless. Then, incredulous, she began to hurry after him.

"Please!—Wait!" she cried. People turned and stared at her as she pushed her way through the crowds: but within seconds he was out of sight, lost irretrievably in the throng of afternoon shoppers. The precious questionnaire was gone for ever!

For a few minutes the disappointment was so overwhelming that Lydia could have sat there on the kerbside and burst into tears. Her marvellous interview, fully and correctly administered to a man of exactly the right age and class—it was all wasted, lost beyond recall! So shattered was she by the disappointment that she hardly bothered to wonder at the man's strange behaviour.

Nor did the Team seem to wonder at it, when they all met at the end of the day to compare notes and hand in their work to the supervisor.

"Oh, it's always happening!" pretty Mrs Robens assured her airily. "They're all nuts, the ones who actually answer. Well, I mean, no one *would* if they were sane, would they?" Approving laughter from the little group. "You should have seen my M.60!" she went on cheerfully.

THE FATED INTERVIEW

"He was a DE if ever there was one, but since he *said* he was the Duke of Wellington and lived at Buckingham Palace, what could I do but put him down as an AB? Especially as I wanted an AB to finish my quota. They won't bat an eyelid, you see!"

All very well for pretty Mrs Robens. She had at least kept hold of her mad interview and could add it to her quota. All very well for her, too, to be hurrying off now to cook chops and asparagus for her adoring husband and to tell him funny stories of her day. All of them, all except Lydia, hurrying home now to their other lives, their real lives, in the context of which all this was a joke, a trifle, an amusing source of evening conversation.

The long evening light was still soft and golden in the street when Lydia let herself into her little room where the sun never shone. Even now, in July, it felt dank and clammy; Lydia switched on the light, and shivered, and sat down wearily in the ugly, uncomfortable armchair. Sat down to wait, to rest her swollen feet, to fill in the hours till it should be time to go to bed.

And then, with the coming of the long night, her real life began; her life of sobbing into her lumpy pillow and thinking about Clive. His selfishness, his cowardice, his short-sighted greed were all Paula's now; and if the girl had owned all the riches of the whole earth, Lydia could not have envied her more, or wept more bitter tears....

At first, Lydia thought the supervisor was hissing at her like a snake: "Miss-sssss S-ssssteele, there's a dis-sssss-crepancy in every s-ssssingle one.... You've s-spoiled the whole s-sssurvey, Miss-sss S-sssteele...."

Lydia struggled up through the deep layers of sleep, and knew that, after all, it was not the supervisor speaking She was alone, in bed, in the deep night, in her dingy, solitary room. Or was she alone? The sense that something was happening, something was wrong, began to stir deep inside her. She struggled to wake, to think, but drowsiness came at her like a breaking wave, hurling her back into some strange uneasy limbo. She lay very still.

There was no sound, except this quiet hissing; yet somehow Lydia knew that there *had* been another sound. Somewhere back among her dreams, there had been an uneasiness in among the furniture, across the linoleum, and then a softly closing door. Yet still she lay, heavy with uninterest: perhaps when she next opened her eyes it would be morning? Perhaps it was nearly morning already? The blank square of window would tell her, by its faint shade of lighter or darker grey, whether the dawn were breaking. Reluctantly, she forced her eyes open.

For a moment, she thought she had gone blind. No grey square, neither dark nor light, was to be seen! Suddenly, crazily awake, she stared up and stared round into the blackness in all directions. Blackness everywhere, black, black, and a singing in her head.... She must have light, light! Light to breathe as well as light to see! Light to dispel this strange feeling in her lungs! Wildly, she reached out to her bedside lamp, and in a moment all was bright and sharp as in a vision. The curtains, which she always left open, were drawn close across the window; and an envelope, white and oblong, was propped against the alarm clock. And still the hissing sound went softly on, relentlessly, as the gas poured steadily from the unlit fire.

With her last strength, Lydia stumbled across the room to turn it off, flung open the window and leaned out, taking in great gulps of the still night air.

And when the dawn came, and her head cleared, she turned back into the room and opened the strange envelope. Inside it, in her own writing, was the message:

"Life has no more meaning—I've lost everything that made living worth while. All I want is to make an end to it all."

Would anyone else who might have found it have realized that the slip of paper had been cut, neatly, from the end of a Market Research questionnaire?

But why? Why? What could the strange man she had interviewed that afternoon have had against her? And why had his face seemed faintly familiar....

The answer came nearly a week later, when she learned that the death of an uncle had left her a rich woman—and that the legacy would have gone, in the event of her death, to a second cousin, a man of fifty-five whom she had not met since he was in his twenties and she a little girl. An ingenious way, she reflected wryly, of getting a suicide note in her own handwriting! And as to the motive, not one of her friends would have been in doubt—Clive, and his heartless desertion.

Clive. A little smile quivered on Lydia's lips as she

thought of Clive's face when it came to his ears that his discarded Lydia was now an extremely rich woman. He would quickly discover that Paula after all did not really understand him; that they were not really suited to each other; that Lydia was after all his own true love.

And wasn't she? The smile broadened on Lydia's lips; it plumped her hollow cheeks, and sparkled up into her defeated eyes. All alone, in her little shabby room, Lydia began to dance.

For when a woman can no longer hope to be loved for her beauty, or her youth, or her charm, is it so small a thing to learn that she may yet be loved for her money?

THE LOCKED ROOM

A DOOR BANGED in the empty flat upstairs.

Margaret felt her fingers tighten on the covers of her library book, but she refused to look up. As long as she could keep her eyes running backward and forward along the lines of print, she could tell herself that she hadn't given in to her fear—to this ridiculous, unreasoning fear that had so inexplicably laid hold of her this evening.

What was there to be afraid of, anyway? Simply that the upstairs flat had been empty all this week, and that Henry was on duty tonight? But she had often been alone before—if you could call it alone, with Robin and Peter in bed in the very next room. Two little boys of six and eight sound asleep in bed can't really be called company, but still ...

Leonora hesitated, wondering which way she should turn.

Margaret realized that she was still reading the same sentence, over and over again, and she shut the book with an angry little slam. What *was* the matter with her? Was it that murder in the papers—some woman strangled by a poor wretch who had been ill-treated in his childhood? He had a grudge against women, or something—Margaret hadn't followed it very carefully—had locked himself in an empty room in this woman's house, and then, in the middle of the night, had crept out...

All very horrid, of course; but then one was always reading of murders in the papers—anyway, they'd probably caught him by now. Now, what had she better do to put these silly ideas out of her head once and for all?

Go upstairs, of course. Go upstairs to the empty flat, look briskly through all the rooms, shut firmly whichever door it was that was banging, and come down again, her mind set at rest. Simple.

She put her book down on the little polished table at her side. But why was she putting it down so softly, so cautiously? Margaret shook herself irritably. There wasn't the slightest need to be quiet. Nothing ever seemed to wake the boys once they were properly off, and poor deaf old Mrs Palmer on the ground floor certainly wouldn't be troubled.

Just to convince herself, she picked the book up again and dropped it noisily on the table. Then, with a firm step, she walked out to the landing.

The once gracious staircase of the old house curved down into complete blackness. For a moment Margaret was taken aback. Even though old Mrs Palmer was often in bed before ten, she always left the hall light on for the other tenants—perhaps, too, for her own sake, from a deaf woman's natural anxiety not to be shut away in darkness as well as silence.

Margaret stood for a moment, puzzled. Then she

remembered. Of course; the poor old thing had gone off this morning on one of her rare visits to a married niece. Tonight the downstairs flat was empty too.

Margaret was annoyed to feel her palms growing sticky as she gripped the top of the banisters, peering down into the darkness. What on earth difference did it make whether Mrs Palmer was there or not? Even if she was there, she would have been asleep by now, deep, deep in her world of silence, far out of reach of any human voice ... of any screams ...

Snap out of it, girl! Margaret scolded herself. This is what comes of reading mystery stories in the evening instead of catching up with the ironing as I meant to! She turned sharply round and walked across the landing to the other staircase—the dusty, narrower staircase that led to the empty flat above.

The hall stairs were in bad enough repair, goodness knew, but these were worse. As Margaret turned the bend which cut her off from the light of her own landing, she could feel the rotten plaster crumbling under her hands as she felt her way up in the darkness.

The pitter-patter of plaster crumbs falling on to the stairboards was a familiar enough sound to Margaret after six months in this decrepit old house; but all the same she wished the little noise would stop. It seemed to make her more nervous—to get in the way of something. And it was only then that she realized how intently her ears were strained to hear some sound from the empty rooms overhead.

But what sound? Margaret stood on the top landing listening for a moment before she reached out for the light switch.

Bother! The owners, who in all these months had never raised a finger to repair rotting plaster, broken locks, and split window frames, had nevertheless bestirred themselves in less than a week to switch off the electric light supply to the vacant flat! Now she would have to explore the place in the dark.

She felt her way along the wall to the first of the four doors that she knew opened on to this landing. It opened easily; and Margaret again silently cursed the owners. If only they'd take the trouble to fix locks on their own property she would have been spared all this—the top flat would have been properly locked up the moment the Davidsons left, and then there would have been no possibility of anyone lurking there. Her annoyance strengthened her, and she flung the door wide open.

Empty, of course. Accustomed as her eyes were to the complete blackness of the landing, the room seemed to be quite brightly lit by the dim square of the window, and she could see at a glance into every empty corner.

The next room was empty too, and the next, except for the twisted, shadowy bulk of the antique gas cooker which Mrs Davidson so often declared had "gone funny on her," and might she boil up a kettle on the slightly newer cooker in Margaret's flat?

But the fourth door *was* locked. Nothing surprising in that, Margaret told herself, turning the shaky china knob this way and that without success. Not surprising at all. All the rooms ought to have been locked like this— probably this was the only one which *would* lock, and the owners had lazily hoped for the best about the others.

THE LOCKED ROOM

A perfectly natural explanation: no need to turn the handle so stealthily ...

To prove the point, Margaret gave the knob a brisk rattle, and it came off in her hand. Just like this house! she was thinking, and heard the corresponding knob on the other side of the door fall to the floor with a report like a pistol in the silence of the night.

But what was *that*? It might have been the echo of the bang, of course, in the empty room. Or—yes, of course, that must be it! Margaret let her breath go in a sigh of relief. That scraping, tapping noise—that was exactly the noise a china knob would make, rolling lopsidedly across the bare boards. Wasn't it?

Yes, of course it was. Margaret was surprised to find how quickly she had got back to her own flat—to her lighted sitting-room—to her own fireside, her heart beating annoyingly, and the dirty china knob still in her hand.

Leonora hesitated, wondering which way she should turn.

Margaret pushed the book away with a gesture of irritation. She had thought that by facing her fear—by going up to the empty flat, looking in all the rooms and shutting the doors firmly so that they couldn't bang, she would have regained her peace of mind. Yet here she was, sitting just as before, her heart thumping, her ears straining for she did not know what.

What *is* it all about? she asked herself. Has anything happened today to make me feel nervous? Have I subconsciously noticed anyone suspicious lurking about outside? God knows it's a queer enough neighbourhood! And leaning her chin on her hands, her thick black curls falling forward on to her damp forehead, she thought over the day.

Absolutely nothing out of the ordinary. Henry had gone to work as usual. The boys had been got off to school with the usual amount of clatter and argument— Peter unable to find his wellingtons, and Robin announcing, at the very last moment, just as they were starting down the steps, that this teacher had said they were all to bring a cardboard box four inches wide and a long thin piece of string.

Then had followed the morning battle for cleanliness against the obstinate old house. The paintwork that collapsed into dry rot if you wiped it too thoroughly. The cobwebs that brought bits of plaster down with them when you got at them with a broom....

They weren't going to be here much longer, that was one thing, reflected Margaret. They would be moving to the country soon after Christmas, and it hadn't seemed worthwhile to look for anywhere else to live for such a short time. Besides, if they *had* to live in a flat with two lively small boys, this ramshackle old place offered some advantages. Among all this decay no one was going to notice sticky fingermarks and more chipped paint; no one was going to complain about what games the children played in the neglected garden, overgrown with brambles and willow herb. No one minded their boots, and the boots of their numerous small friends, clattering up and down the stairs.

Margaret smiled as she thought of the odd assortment

of friends her sons had managed to collect during their six months here. Such a queer mixture of children in a neighbourhood like this, ranging from real little street toughs to the bespectacled son of a divorced but celebrated professor. Always in and out of the house—Margaret couldn't put a name to half of them. That crowd this afternoon, for instance—who *were* they all?

Margaret wrinkled her brows, trying to remember. Alan, of course, the freckle-faced mischief from the paper shop at the corner. And Raymond—the fair, sly boy that Henry said she shouldn't let the children play with—but what could you do? And William—stodgy, mouse-coloured William—who simply came to eat her cakes, it seemed to Margaret, for he never played at anything in particular with the others.

Oh, and there had been another one today—a new one, for whom Margaret had felt an immediate revulsion. About eight or nine he must have been, very small for his age and yet strangely mature, with a sharp, shrewd light in his pale, red-rimmed eyes. He had a coarse mop of ill-cut ginger hair and the palest of pale eyebrows and eyelashes, almost invisible in his pale, pinched face. And he was painfully thin.

In spite of her dislike, Margaret had been touched by the thinness—and puzzled, too—real undernourishment is so rare in children nowadays. She had pressed on him cakes and bread and jam, but he had not eaten anything —indeed, he seemed scarcely aware that anything was being offered him—and in the end Margaret had given up and let the others demolish the provisions with their usual speed.

Margaret shivered, suddenly cold, and leaned forward to put more coal on the fire. The memory of this queer, ginger-haired child had somehow made her feel uneasy all over again. She wished she'd made more effort to find out who he was and where he came from, but the boys were always so vague about that sort of thing.

"What, Mummy?" Peter had said when she had asked him about the child that evening; "Mummy, you said *I* could have the next corn-flake packet, and now Robin ..."

"Yes, yes, darling, but listen. Who was that little ginger-haired boy you brought home from school today?"

"Who did?" interrupted Robin helpfully.

"Well—Peter, I suppose. Or do *you* know him, Robin? Perhaps he's *your* friend?"

"Who is?"

Margaret had sighed. "The little ginger-haired boy. The one who hardly ate anything at tea."

"*I* didn't hardly eat anything, either," remarked Robin smugly.

"Ooo—you story!" broke in Peter indignantly. "I saw you myself, you had three cakes, and ..."

Margaret had given it up, and determined to ask the child himself if he ever turned up again.

And, strangely enough, as she had gone across their own landing to put on the boys' bath, she thought she caught a glimpse of the little creature in the hall below, darting past the foot of the stairs. But she couldn't be sure; dusk always fell early in that dim, derelict hall, and the whole thing might have been a trick of the light. Anyway, when she had gone to the back door and called into the damp autumn twilight, there had been no answer, and nothing stirred among the rank, overgrown shrubs and weeds.

Margaret picked up her book again, slightly reassured. All this could quite reasonably explain her nervousness tonight. She was feeling guilty, that's what it must be. There was something peculiar about the child, and she should have made more effort to find out about him. Perhaps he needed help—after all, there *were* cases of child cruelty and neglect even nowadays. Tomorrow she would really go into the matter, and then there would be nothing more to worry about.

Leonora hesitated, wondering which way she should turn.

Sometimes, on waking from a deep sleep, one knows with absolute certainty that something has wakened one, but without knowing what. Margaret knew, with just this certainty, that something had made her raise her eyes from the book. She listened—listened as she had listened before that night—to the deep pulsing in her ears, to the tiny flickering murmur of the coals. Nothing more.

But wasn't there? What was that, then, that faint, faint shuffle on the landing outside? Shuffle, shuffle, soft as an autumn leaf drifting—shuffle shuffle—pad pad ... silently the door swung open and there stood Robin, blinking, half asleep.

Margaret let out her breath in a gasp of relief.

"Robin! Whatever's the matter? Why aren't you asleep?"

Robin blinked at her owlishly, his eyes large and round

as they always were when just wakened from sleep.

"I don't like that little boy in my bed," he observed.

"What little boy? Whatever are you talking about, Robin?"

"That little boy. He's horrid. He pinches me. And he's muddling the blankets. On purpose."

"Darling, you're dreaming! Come along and let's see!"

Taking the child's hand, Margaret led him back into his own room and switched on the light.

There was Peter, rosily asleep with his mouth open as usual; and there was Robin's little bed, empty, and with the clothes tumbled this way and that as if he had tossed about a lot in his sleep.

This confirmed Margaret's opinion that he had had a nightmare. After all, what was more likely after her cross-questioning about the mysterious little visitor that evening? In spite of his apparent inattention, Robin had no doubt sensed something of the anxiety and distaste behind her questions, and it was the most likely thing in the world that he would dream about it when he went to bed.

However, to reassure the child, Margaret embarked on a thorough search of the little room. Under both the beds they looked, into the clothes closet, behind the curtains—even, at Robin's insistence, into the impossibly narrow space behind the chest of drawers.

"He was such a *thin* little boy, you see, Mummy," Robin explained, and the phrase gave Margaret a nasty little pang of uneasiness. The hungry, too-old little face seemed to hover before her for a moment, its eyes full of ancient, malicious knowledge. She blinked it away, shut the lid of the brick box (what an absurd place to look!), and bundled Robin firmly back to bed.

"And do you promise I won't dream it again?" asked Robin anxiously, and Margaret promised. This was the standard formula after Robin's nightmares. It had always worked before.

Nearly twelve o'clock. There was nothing whatever to stay up for, but somehow Margaret couldn't bring herself to go to bed. She reached out towards her library book, but felt that she could not face Leonora's indecision again, and instead picked up yesterday's evening paper. She would look for something cheerful to read before she went to bed. The autumn fashions, perhaps—or would it be the spring ones they'd be writing about in October? It was all very confusing nowadays.

But it wasn't the autumn fashions she found herself reading—or the spring ones. It was the blurred photograph of the wanted man that caught her eye—a man in his fifties perhaps—from such a bad picture it was difficult to tell. A picture of the murdered woman, too—a Mrs Harriet somebody—and a description of her ...

Margaret's attention suddenly became riveted and she read the report from beginning to end, hardly daring to breathe. This man, at large somewhere in London tonight, had escaped from a mental institution where he had been sent some years ago for strangling another woman in somewhat similar circumstances to this Mrs Harriet ...

Margaret felt her limbs grow rigid. Both women had been the mothers of small boys ... both had lived in tall derelict houses converted into flats ... both had had black hair done in tight curls ... Margaret fingered her hairstyle with damp, trembling fingers, and tried not to read any more, but her eyes seemed glued to the page. Why had the man not been hanged that first time?

There followed the story of his childhood—a story of real Dickensian horror. Brought up in a tall ruined old house by a stepmother who had starved him, thrashed him, shut him in dark rooms where she told him clawed fiends were waiting ... her black, shining curls had quivered over his childhood like the insignia of torture and death. The prison doctors had learned all this from him after the first murder—and had learned, too, how the sight of a black-haired woman going up the steps of just such a derelict house as he remembered had brought back his terror and misery with such vividness that "I didn't just *feel* like a little boy again—I *was* a little boy ... that was my house ... that was *her*"—that was the only way he could describe it. And he had crept into the house, locked himself in one of the empty rooms until the dead silence of the night, and then crept out, with a child's enormity of terror and hatred in his heart, and with a man's strength in his fingers ...

Margaret closed her eyes for a second, and then opened them again to read the description of the murderer: "About fifty years of age, medium height, ginger hair growing grey, eyebrows and eyelashes almost invisible ..." With every word the face leaped before her more vividly —not the face of the ageing, unknown man, but the little malevolent face she had seen that afternoon—the ill-cut ginger hair, the little red-rimmed eyes filled with the twisted malice of an old and bitter man ...

"I didn't just *feel* like a little boy again, I *was* a little boy ..." The words beat through Margaret's brain, over and over again.

She thrust the paper away from her. Don't be so fanciful and absurd, she told herself. After all, if I *really* think anything's wrong all I've got to do is call the police. There's the telephone just there in the hall.

She walked slowly to the door and out on to the landing, and stood there in her little island of light with darkness above and below. She tried to go on telling herself what nonsense it all was, how ridiculous she was being. But now she dared not let any more words come into her mind, not any words at all. For she was listening—listening as civilized human beings rarely have need to listen—listening as an animal listens in the murderous blackness of the forest. Not just with the ears—rather with the whole body. Every organ, every nerve is alert, pricked up, so that, in the end, it is impossible to say through which sense the message comes, and comes with absolute certainty: Danger is near. Danger is on the move.

For there was no sound. Margaret was certain of that. No sound to tell her that something was stirring in the locked room upstairs—that dark, empty room so like the locked room where once a little boy had gone half mad with terror at the thought of the clawed fiends. The clawed fiends who had lost their terrors through the years and become his friends and allies, for now at last he was a clawed fiend himself.

Still Margaret heard no sound. No sound to tell that the door of the empty room was being unlocked, silently, and with consummate skill, from the inside. No shuffle of footsteps across the dusty upstairs landing. No creak from the ancient, rickety steps of that top flight of stairs.

And in the end it was not Margaret's straining ears at all which caught the first hint of the oncoming creature—it was her eyes. They seemed to have been riveted on that shadowy bend in the banisters for so long that when she saw the hand at last, long and tapering, like five snakes coiled round the rail, she could have imagined it had been there all the time, flickering in and out and dancing before her eyes.

But not the face. No, that couldn't have been there before. Not anywhere, in all the world, could there have been a face like that—a face so distorted, so alight with hate that it seemed almost luminous as it leered out of the blackness, as it seemed to glide down towards her a foot or two above the banister...

There was a sound now—a quick pattering of feet, horribly light and soft, like a child's, as they bore the heavy adult shape down the stairs, the white, curled fingers reaching out towards her...

A little frightened cry at Margaret's elbow freed her from her paralysis. A little white face, a tangle of ginger hair ... and an instinct stronger that that of self-preservation gripped her. In a second she was on her knees, her arms round the small trembling body; she felt the little creature's shaking terror subsiding into a great peace as she held him against her breast.

That dropping on her knees was her salvation. In that very second her assailant lunged, tripped over her suddenly lowered body, and pitched headlong down the stairs behind her. Crash upon crash as he fell from step to step, and then silence. Absolute silence.

Then a new clamour arose:

"Mummy! Mummy! Who...? What...?"—a tangle of small legs and arms, and in a moment her arms seemed to be full of little boys. She collected her wits and looked down at them. Only two of them, of course, her own two, their familiar dark heads pressed against her, their frightened questions clamouring in her ears ...

And when the police came, and Henry came, and the dead man was taken away, there was so much to tell. So much to explain. It could all be explained quite easily, of course (as Henry pointed out), with only a little stretching of coincidence.

The little ginger-headed boy must come from somewhere in the neighbourhood—no doubt he could be traced, and if necessary helped in some way. Margaret's obsession about him would explain Robin's dream; it would also explain why, in that moment of terror, she imagined the strange child had rushed into her arms. Really, of course, it must have been one of her own boys.

And yet, Margaret could never forget the smile on the face of the dead man as he lay crumpled at the foot of the stairs. They say that the faces of the dead can set in all sorts of incongruous expressions, but it seemed to Margaret that the smile had not been the smile of a grown man at all; it had been the smile of a little boy who has felt the comfort of a mother's arms at last.